I0623000

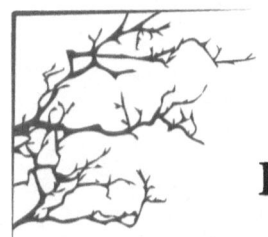

Dedication

TO AARON AND SIERRA - my two amazing children. You both provide more love in my life than I ever could imagine.

This story is for you ... I hope one day you both will have the courage to do what is right, especially if odds aren't in your favor. As long as you stick together, anything is possible.

Never give up, Never surrender, Never quit.

THE ONES WHO LIVED
By
Ashley Nemer

ART OF SAFKHET

THE ONES WHO LIVED
Cover Design by Ashley Nemer
Photo Credit: Rain By Isoga
Edited by Andrea's Proofreading
Format by Ashley Nemer
Copyright © Ashley Nemer 2018
All rights reserved.

ISBN 13: 978-1-941194-12-6

A product of the
Art of Safkhet
Published September, 2018

Author's Note

DYSTOPIAN STORIES ALWAYS are critiqued and compared to epic stories like *The Hunger Games* and *1984*. What I have always thought was missing was the beginning. The start. People at some point wake up and realize life has changed and now we have to deal with the consequences. This story starts at that point, the point where *The Ones Who Lived* realize they are now on their own and life will forever be changed.

This story doesn't have the epic battles and strife that seventy-five years of wars bring out to the surface. It doesn't have the tyranny of leaders that are scared of an educated populace. This story has death, the death of family. The death of hope, the death of a future.

My story has the beginning. I hope that as you read about Anthony and Amelia you look at it from that mindset. Put yourself in their shoes, seventeen and frightened. What would you do? How would you handle it?

Enjoy *The Ones Who Lived* and make note, one day, maybe you will have to perform these tasks yourselves.

Ashley

P.S. For an easy reference point, this books starting point takes place in August 2017 right after the Solar Eclipse, Hurricane Harvey and the wild fires in California.

TABLE OF
CONTENTS

August 21st, 2017 ...
The World Darkens

When the earth becomes dark for minutes at a time
When the waters pour from the sky with no end in sight
When the fire engulfs the land and trees
Death will be here
When the ocean opens up and pours itself on land
When the forests burn all in its path
When the sun vanishes from everyone's eyes
Death will be here
Death will be here to all who are missing the trait
Death will be here to all who are not defining the fate
Death Death Death becomes everyone
Death to all who stand in the way
Death

Prequel - The Day
Before Death...

THE SOUND OF THE DING from his phone alerted him to a notification. Anthony peered down at his cellphone and saw his sister had finally responded to the AP test question he had asked her two hours ago. There can be times when she drove him nuts! She wouldn't intentionally give him the answer to the exam they had both studied for together. Amelia's high moral ground tended to get under his skin, but that didn't matter. The next day their dad will be home from his week away, and they had planned before he left to spend this weekend fishing.

Being the son of a pilot didn't wield a lot of advantages, except when it came to vacation season. Consistent and hard work were the tools he used to gain his father's attention. His father seemed too busy most of the time to help.

Amelia seemed like she belonged in a different lifetime. She looked at her relationship with her father as if it's a grain of salt. One where kids weren't as dependent on their parents for every little detail. Anthony thought of his sister as superior, never requiring the constant need for approval. At the same time, she missed out on a lot of the bonding that he and their dad got during his off days, unless they were out hunting. Amelia and her dad loved to hunt together..

Being a twin brought along many advantages, like always having a best friend. But even still, sometimes Anthony and Amelia gave off the perception like they were separate beings. His sister did all sorts of things he never would consider fun, but then again, she was a girl and he was a guy.

Without thinking about the consequences of the room he was sitting in, he pulled his cell phone back out from his pocket and shot Sam, his best friend, a quick text.

Hey man, tonight you want to come over, dad's coming home we need to get the gear ready.

Seconds ticked by, and Anthony waited for the delivered message to be read.

"Anthony, can you tell me the answer?"

He quickly brought his head forward and acknowledged his math teacher while she spoke to him. She was pointing to the quadratic equation on the front white board and wanting him to solve it.

"Um, sure, yes ma'am."

With a pen and paper in hand, he took to working out the problem using the formula on the board, but when the bell rang he obtained instant relief, because he was fairly positive he was doing it wrong. Without much thought, he gathered his papers and books up, and walked to the front of the classroom where he bumped Sam on the shoulder.

"You see my text?"

Sam moved his head back and forth, "No man, I kept it in my locker. My mom's gonna skin me alive if she gets one more phone call about me and my cell during school hours."

"Oh, well you wanna come over tonight? I have to get the supplies ready for my dad coming home tomorrow."

"Can't, I'm babysitting my little cousin today and then tomorrow after school. My aunt and uncle are going out on the town two nights in a row. My mom says her sister is reclaiming her youth, whatever that means."

"Dang bro, hope they are paying you."

"No, but that's alright. She isn't too bad to be around. And it makes me appear awesome too, and since Christmas is right around the corner I figure the good will couldn't hurt anything."

"Ha, right on man. Okay, well, possibly this weekend we can do something."

"Will Amy be there?"

"Duh, she lives there doesn't she?"

Anthony snapped his head around to observe his friend for a split second and thought he desired to get with his sister, but he let those images pass, no way would he break that guy code.

With a sensation of nostalgia, Anthony gazed around at the bricks racing down the corridor, the halls in his high school were narrow and long. Lots of twists and turns, the freshman always got lost. This was their senior year, soon they would be free of the confines of adults and his life would take on a whole new start. Amelia, Sam and he talked about it frequently, life outside of Hill Tree High.

"Anthony, you're going to be late for class." The principal said to him as he walked up beside him in the hallway.

"No sir, heading there right now!" He brought his arm up and pointed to the open doorway ten feet ahead of him.

"Good job son make sure you focus."

Exemplifying how a father should be, Principal Jones was always trying to be a role model to everyone. Sometimes it was cool, other times like today it was just annoying. "Yes sir. Bye!"

Without a second thought Anthony rushed into the classroom and took his seat right as the bell was starting to ring.

Anthony glanced at his watch on his left wrist and grinned, the day was almost over, forty-five minutes remaining, and he would be heading home.

THE CAR RIDE HOME WAS a snooze fest. Amelia essentially ignored Anthony the whole way home from school. She had one thing on her mind and one thing only, Sam. Today in biology class they had touched hands twice while doing the experiment and that had never happened before. Her mind wouldn't let it go, she kept thinking about it.

Amelia's feelings for Sam were jumbled, unable to determine if she truly liked him like that. He was her brother's best friend and her friend. Friends didn't touch hands. Did they?

"Amy! Are you paying attention?"

Anthony's voice brought her back into the present and she shook her head back and forth. "Sorry bro, lots on my mind, long day."

"Yeah long day for me too, considering that test in class today. Which by the way, thanks for giving me the heads up on the AP History test."

"I told you I would refuse to cheat, and besides, you knew the answer."

"Not the point, sis. You're supposed to help a brother out."

"Expressions like that just aren't applicable in these situations, but I will make a noted for next time."

"I hate AP History. I don't see why I have to take it, I'll never use it."

"Because mom knows you're smart enough, don't you love learning about all the interesting things from our worlds past?"

"Not really it will never even be used."

"Sure it will, I imagine you've heard the saying that history always repeats itself."

Anthony peered over at Amelia as he pulled their car into the driveway. "Alright smarty pants, when are we ever going to need to apply the Middle Ages knowledge in modern times?"

Amelia smiled, "Simple, if we want to keep the Black Death away we will always pay our sewer usage fees."

Anthony rolled his eyes at her and got out of the car, Amelia lingered for a second or two longer than she needed, before joining him at the front door. "I worry about you Anthony."

"And I worry about you too Amelia. Come on let's go inside and see if we can sneak some of the desert for tomorrow that we know mom is hiding from us."

"Deal."

Every issue has a silver lining supposedly, well having a twin always meant one thing, there was a partner in every crime that could be trusted.

"Hey Anthony, did you notice anything strange about the weather today?"

Wind whirled past Amelia when she began looking up at the clouds, they formed clusters to make different mountainous swirls in the air in a pattern she had never seen before. She wasn't sure why this bothered her so much, but something about it made her stomach feel like it had just survived a roller coaster.

"I don't know, what do you mean strange?"

"Look at the clouds, that doesn't seem strange to you?"

"You are aware that hurricane season is here. We just had a huge storm here, of course the clouds are going to be weird."

"I suppose so, maybe you're right."

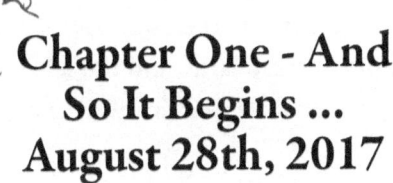

Chapter One - And So It Begins ... August 28th, 2017

AMELIA AND ANTHONY were on their way home from school when out of nowhere Amelia noticed an airplane out of the passenger side window plummeting to the Earth. The two teenagers never before had witnessed a car crash let alone a plane barreling down to the earth. The sound and sight of the explosion that occurred off to the right side of their view took the siblings' breaths away.

"Dad wasn't on that plane right?" Amelia asked her brother.

"No, he was supposed to be home hours ago. Mom said he would be home before we got back from school." Anthony's words were reassuring but his tone was saddened. No one could watch lives plummet to their death and not be struck by the horror and sadness of that.

"You're positive right Anthony?"

"Yeah Amy I am, I'm positive Dad's at home."

Obvious signs developed in the sky, it turned black and the air became dense, the humidity was sweltering, the temperature rose at an exponential rate. Thunder rumbled through the air and lightning swarmed the sky. The storm brewing was fiercer than any others that Saint Pete had experienced before.

The storm developed so briskly that Anthony and Amelia made it home in time to seek shelter out of the storm. The neighborhood traffic seemed eerily quiet. The streets held cars on either side, yet no one was driving. The green lawns were empty, not even the neighbors in their yards, and the sense of doom hung overhead as they pulled into their driveway and got out of their car.

"Mom, you home?" Anthony called out, as he and his twin sister ran into the house from the garage. Dinner was set out on the table as well as every light flipped in the on position.

"Momma you won't believe what Anthony did!" Amelia shouted, while she dropped her purse and jacket on the kitchen table.

"Where do you think they are, mom left us food?" Anthony questioned his sister.

"Who knows maybe they made plans together. Let's eat and enjoy a movie."

His sister never cared about the innate details all her focus centered on the end result. Anthony worried about everything. His levels of anxiety always bothered his parents, but they never found a solution for his tendencies to carry the world on his shoulders.

"She made Dad's favorite." The lasagna smelled amazing and both twins' stomachs growled with hunger. The last meal they consumed was lunch, while at school near eleven this morning. Supper time being six hours later, they anxiously awaited dinner.

In a sarcastic tone Anthony said, "Dad came home today from his trip don't you remember?" Anthony pulled two plates out of the cupboard and set them down on the kitchen table.

"Wonder how long he will be staying home this time. Dad made his job appear like he is always flying away overnight. He promised me a weekend fishing trip so hopefully that means he will be here until Monday."

"He's a pilot Anthony, what do you expect Dad to do, fly only eight hours a day?" Amelia grabbed the silverware their mom had left on the kitchen island and set them next to the plates her brother had set out.

"Yes, precisely, that's I expect." His response was simple and straight forward.

An exaggerated sigh left her lips and the eye roll that Amelia gave her brother made him go into a tirade over this topic. It became an ongoing conversation in their household between their parents. Mom wanted their dad home more and their dad wanted their mom to enjoy his high paying salary and to enjoy life.

"Where are they?" Anthony said while he walked around the living room and dining room. "Mom's purse is sitting in her chair in the living room, she wouldn't have left without it."

Amelia walked toward the hall closet and opened the door, she recognized her father's brief case. "Anthony! Dad's brief case is in the closet, and his wallet is on the table. He's home!" Her voice was more of the volume of a scream than a loud comment. The twins were now frantic and running through the house calling or their parent.

"I found them!" Anthony hollered from their bedroom closet. His voice contained a level of fear and panic that Amelia didn't know how to process. Her heart sped up, increasing the thumps she detect inside her head.

The stairs moved quickly under her shoes as she took them two at a time. Amelia came running into the room and the second she viewed her brother's face she understood whatever he found would end poorly. Tears began to form in her eyes as she shook her head back and forth. "No, no, Anthony no!" She started to cry and fell to the floor. Her brother crossed the room and wrapped his arms around his sister and pulled her close.

"Their dead. I don't," he stopped talking to catch his breath and take in what he was about to say. "I don't know how." Tears streaked his cheeks while he rocked back and forth with his sister, holding her close. Neither of them spoke, they simply sat, motionless as if they had died too. The air in the room had not come to a point where the smell of a dead body was evident, but Amelia didn't want to risk that being the next phase.

"We need to call the police. They must have been murdered but I didn't see any blood." Anthony protested to his sister.

"Perhaps they aren't dead, did you check for a pulse?" Amelia's anxiousness picked up as she stood and walked towards the closet.

"No, I didn't touch them" Anthony walked behind her slowly. He watched her kneel beside their mother and place her two fingers along her neck and then his mom's wrist. He knew she didn't find a pulse, he was right they left this world on a new journey alone, without them.

"Anthony call the police." His sister's voice was firm, and it set him into motion. He pulled out his cell phone and dialed nine-one-one.

"Something's wrong." He said to Amelia. "No one is picking up."

"Someone always answer at the police station." She stated.

"Yep, pretty sure the sole purpose of switch board is to answer. I'm trying again, and no one is picking up."

Amelia checked their father's body for a pulse, and once again came up short. "What about Uncle Mack?"

"Good idea, he's a doctor he can tell us if they were murdered." He pulled his number up on his cell phone and pressed call. When his voicemail picked up he left a message and then ended the call. "Left a message. He's probably in surgery or something."

"I can't sit here and let them stay like this." Amelia said. She moved her head in all directions, looking around for something specifically she needed.

"We have to, we can't move them, and the police need to see how they, the bodies, got discovered." Anthony walked to his sister and pulled her into a standing position, he focused her attention to look at him. "We have to be smart about this, because we can't be the ones to mess the scene up."

"Mess the scene up, what are you CSI?" She laughed slightly at the comment, their whole family had teased Anthony about how much he loved crime shows and watched all that he could on television. But currently, he was right, he knew more about what to expect than she did, and Amelia didn't want to hurt anything that could help.

The two of them walked down the stairwell and into the kitchen. Anthony tried to call the police again but same as before no one answered and something in his gut told him this night was the first of many long nights. Amelia refused to accept reality, she took a single look at her brother and ran for the front door.

"Amy! Where are you going?" Anthony ran after her.

"I can't do this I can't! There are planes falling from the sky and our parents are dead!" The sound of her frantic voice traveled through the air. Anthony chased her, followed her, through their street, as she banged on doors yelling for anyone to help.

"What are we going to do?" His sister looked at him with worry in her eyes and fear in her voice. Her brother had finally caught up to her when she paused to breathe back in their drive way.

"We will get through this together. Whatever 'this' may be. Okay?"

All she could do was nod at him, there was zero reassurance given in this gesture. "Maybe whoever did this will come back and try to hurt us, should we prepare?"

"I don't think so, I mean, if they wanted us they could have had us at any time since we came home. Amy we're safe."

"You don't know that, I'm going to get Dad's gun." She turned towards their house and began her ascent into their home with Anthony trailing behind her.

"We don't have the safe code." He declared.

"I do, I saw him type it in a long time ago and memorized it." She turned and ran off into the den. When she returned to the kitchen she was holding two rifles and a handgun. "Here, you take a rifle."

"This is a bit overkill don't you think?" Anthony checked the rifle to make sure there wasn't anything in the chamber and then placed it on the table top.

"Nope, I am not going to be taken by surprise like Mom and Dad clearly were."

"Well I hope someone calls me back soon. While you were gone I called Grandpa and left a message with him too."

"He is going to be crushed, Mom was all he had left." Amelia loaded her rifle and cocked the bullet into the chamber. "But we will be there for him."

"It kinda creeps me out that you are so comfortable with Dad's rifle."

"He loved to go hunting with me. He wanted you to join us every time we went Anthony." Her voice lowered as she said that, he would never get the opportunity to hunt with their father now. At seventeen they became orphans and everything that populated their lives became altered forever.

Anthony's cell phone went off and both twins jumped. He looked at the name that showed up on the front screen of the phone and he shook his head at Amelia. "Hey Sam, can't talk right now." The tears still streamed from his eyes. He did everything possible to keep the panic at bay.

"What, what do you mean?" He paused and listened to his friend talk and then responded, "Us too, I walked into the bedroom and discovered their bodies. What the hell man? Maybe our folks spent time together and made the same enemy?" Anthony knew his logic was flawed and merely reaching for an answer. What other solution could be true? What other solution could be more likely?"

"Anthony what's going on?" Amelia pestered at her brother. She could see the look in his eyes, she knew it was more bad news, this time it was for their best friend.

"Sam's parents are dead too and he can't get ahold of the police either."

"How can four people suddenly die at the same time? And don't forget the airplane falling to the ground." Amelia asked rhetorically.

"Sam why don't you and Sunny come over. We are better off as four instead of two."

"Four?" Amelia stated in the form of a question, she's aware that Sam was an only child.

"His cousin is at his house, he was going to babysit her tonight. He doesn't want a six-year-old to see his dead parents."

"Makes sense, tell them we have food." She had always heard that women had to remain strong for their men. That saying was going to be put to the test tonight.

Anthony nodded and walked into another room and continued talking to Sam. Amelia stayed in the kitchen and now felt like she could focus on a purpose. She looked around at the food her mother diligently made and decided she would finish setting the table for their impending guests. Their two guest rooms already contained sheets, so Sam and his little cousin could stay in their own rooms comfortably. She could do this, she must keep things together.

"Sam will be here with Sunny in five minutes he was going to take his mom's car and come over."

"Does he even have a license yet?" She asked her brother. She noticed that her hands begun to shake, she almost felt like she was getting sick. Cold sweats were starting to cause her to shiver. Amelia had to focus on something, focus on anything.

"I am absolutely sure in moments like this, those small technicalities don't exactly matter. More so when the police aren't even answering the phone."

"Good point. I'm scared Anthony." she admitted in a voice full of anxiety.

"Me to sis, but we will manage. Okay?"

She nodded at her brother and then focused on cutting the lasagna into even squares. She made some lemonade and as her new reality started to sink in tears began to form in her eyes once again. The tears fell down her cheeks at the same time the doorbell rang.

"Got it!" Anthony yelled as he ran out of the kitchen and into the entryway.

Voices drifted through the downstairs and she couldn't make out a lot of words, but she could detect the sound of a little girl crying. She cleaned her hands off on the towel on the counter and then walked into the room and knelt in front of Sam's cousin.

"Hi sweetie, I'm Amelia, you can call me Amy. What's your name?"

"Sunny." She said as she wiped her tears off on her sleeve.

"Well Sunny, I bet you're hungry, I have some food in the kitchen. Do you want to eat?"

She nodded, and Amelia glanced up at Sam and smiled, "I'll take care of her, you two talk."

"Thanks Amy," Sam said calmly.

"No problem Sam, I got her."

When the two girls left the room, Sam shook his head back and forth and then said, "I can't get ahold of Sunny's parents. I left messages with them and the rest of our family members in a ninety-mile area. No answers."

"Man, this isn't good. My sister pulled out two rifles and a handgun she's afraid someone will come back and try to kill us like they did our parents."

"My folks don't have any gunshot or stab wounds, no blood, nothing that looks like an attack took place."

"Same here, it's the weirdest thing."

"What do you think it means?" Sam looked at the rifle on the couch and smiled as he shook his head, "Man, your sister is a trip."

Anthony chuckled and nodded, "She is something else, but I think there has to be a logical explanation for this."

"This rain storm outside is getting scary, there could be power outages if it keeps up all night."

"Got that covered, our dad instilled solar panels on our roof and a solar generator in the back yard in case of emergencies. So, we're gonna be set."

"Dang man, it's like your own little compound." Sam walked to the chair and sat down. "Thanks for letting us come over."

"I don't think we wanted to be alone anyway and Amy does better when she has something to do, Sunny will help fill that need."

"Guys, you hungry?" Amelia's voice came from the kitchen.

"We'll be right in." Sam answered.

"I don't know that I can eat," Anthony said.

"It isn't technically about eating but company, I like your sister and she will help make this easier."

"Be careful Sam, she's my baby sister."

"You do know I am aware you're only three minutes older than her, right?"

"Baby sister is a baby sister, do not hurt her."

Sam grinned and saluted his friend, "Will do chief."

The two guys walked into the kitchen to see Amelia and Sunny sitting at the table eating. "Smells good sis."

"Mom made it, so you know it is." She smiled a half smile at him. "Sunny seems to like it."

"It's very good." Sunny said with a grin.

The two guys grabbed a glass of water and sat down at the table where the two untouched plates sat. The four of them ate in silence. No one knew what tomorrow would bring but one thing the four kids knew, odds are better four versus two, and two versus none. So together they would remain.

When it was all said and done, dishes put away and the girls upstairs Sam looked at Anthony, "What are we going to do with our parent's bodies?"

Anthony's face went grim and he regretfully said, "We bury them Sam, tomorrow evening. All six of our parents."

Sam raised an eyebrow up and looked at his friend, "But where?"

The two of them looked at each other silently for a moment before Anthony spoke, "I think when we go on our supply run tomorrow we bring yours and Sunny's folks back here. We find a place in our neighborhood where all six of them can be together."

"Like our back yard?" Sam looked out of the window towards the ground.

"No, like under a tree somewhere, somewhere that isn't going to be used for anything other than remembering our folks."

Sam nodded at his friend and stated, "Agreed. Tomorrow then."

Amelia set Sunny up in the guest room next door to her room. She knew that the little girl was scared, and Sam never gave off the impression of the overly compassionate sort of guy. Amelia, focusing on taking care of Sunny, would give her plenty of things to keep her mind off her dead parents in their room down the hall. Sam's friendship of fifteen years meant she and Anthony knew Sam for almost all of their lives, they went to school together since daycare as toddlers. Plus, another guy in the house made Amelia feel safer, especially since she possessed her father's guns.

The only problem was that she was the only one who knew how to really shoot. There was a gut feeling that told her something seriously bad lurked outside of the walls of her home, something she wouldn't to be able to stand.

The running family joke with her parents always circled back to preparing for the apocalypse, which suddenly didn't seem like much of a joke at all. Amelia tried calling the police again and just as before there was no answer. Along with her grandfather and Uncle Mack. There was something very strange going on and for whatever reason Amelia knew deep in her gut that life for all of them changed and that it would never be the same again. She didn't mean just with being orphans.

"Knock knock" Sam said, as he walked into her room.

"You all settled in?" She said to him in a low tone.

"Yeah, tomorrow I think I am going to drive out to Sunny's parents place and grab some of her things and then go back to my place and grab my stuff. Would you mind watching Sunny?"

"No problem, I like her she is a sweet kid."

"She really is, all little kids tend to bother me but she gets my nerves the least, that's why I don't mind babysitting her."

"Were you able to get a hold of anyone in your family yet?"

Sam shook his head, "No, that's why I don't want her coming with me when I go get her things in case we find the same situation. What do you think she will need?"

"I'll make you a list of stuff. But I certainly think we are better as four instead of two and two. Let's call this place home base since we have the guaranteed power source and your house doesn't."

"Anthony and I already talked about that a bit ago, he is going with me and we're going to pick up supplies from my house to bring here so we are set for a while until we figure out what's going on. We're also going to bring our parents here to bury with yours."

"I think it would be best to leave first thing in the morning, as soon as the sun's out."

Sam tilted his head in question, "Why do you think that?"

"Cause what if my dad ended up being right, and it's the zombie apocalypse now, you don't want to be caught out at night do you?"

Sam bellowed a laugh and shook his head, "Amy, you seriously are just like your dad, always jumping to extremes. But sure, I will leave with Anthony right after breakfast."

"Sleep well Sam." She smirked at her friend.

"You too Amy, I'll be two doors down if you get scared." He winked at her.

Amelia laughed and walked over to him and lightly pushed him out into the hallway, "You're always nothing but trouble.

Goodnight." After she shut the door she inhaled a deep breath, she was scared but she could never really let that show. People depended on her now and it was up to her to make sure everyone was taken care of until they all could figure out what was going on.

Her sleep seemed to go well for the first night without her parents, or as well as it could be. She mostly laid in bed and starred up at the ceiling thinking about the last time she saw her mom and dad. How she knew they loved her, but that life would forever be different now. Most likely Anthony and Sam would find the same thing tomorrow at Sunny's house. Was this why the neighborhood gave off the appearance of being so quiet? What happened that caused people to die and did the killer consider the four of them next?

She wanted to dwell on these things but decided sleep would be a better friend. There was a feeling deep in her gut that this disaster was just getting started and each day would be worse than the last for quite some time.

Something inside her made her pick up her cell phone. Amelia realized she hadn't talked to Charlotte or Kelly, two of her best friends. One was in college; the other went to school and was a senior with her and Anthony. Not letting another second go by she reached out and dialed first Charlotte. The phone rang and rang with no answer. Maybe whatever affected them in Saint Pete didn't affect those up in Tallahassee. Florida State University was far away, it could be possible this was a localized disaster.

Taking a second attempted she clicked on Kelly's name to dial the number. After two rings she heard her friend pick up.

"Amelia, oh my god! This is a disaster!" her friend said in a hysterical voice.

"Calm down Kelly, I take it your parents are dead too?"

"Dead? I don't know. Neither are home and everyone in my neighborhood is losing it. Like, where is everyone?"

"I have no clue, Sam is over here with Anthony and me, all our parents are gone, and we found them in our houses just, gone."

"It's a crisis I tell you, I hope mine are alive."

"Have you spoken to Charlotte yet?" Amelia asked.

"Nope can't get ahold of her, called her earlier before I realized there was some type of calamity happening."

"If you need to come over we have room, I don't want you to be alone."

She could hear Kelly shaking her head on the phone before she spoke again, "No I'm fine, I called Zach up and we are over at his place. I don't know what to make of it but we all need to be careful. Keep in touch okay?"

"Yeah I will, I don't like this at all."

Amelia continued the conversation for another hour. Around three in the morning there was a light knock on her door that jarred Amelia out of her slumber. She saw the door start to open and light shined through the crack.

"Amy, I'm scared." She heard Sunny say in a soft and shaken voice.

"Come in sweetie you can stay with me."

The little girl ran to the bed in a quick step and Amelia barely had enough time to pull the covers back to welcome the young child in with her.

"I don't like not being at my house." She said, while looking up at Amelia with tears in her eyes.

"It's scary I know, but we got to all be brave together Sunny. You have Sam, my brother, and me. We will all look out for you."

"My dad lets me watch The Walking Dead sometimes, is that what is going on outside, are people turning into zombies?"

The question caught Amelia by surprise and it took her a moment to answer it. "God, I hope not, my parents are in their room still. I am pretty sure that zombies can't exist sweetie."

"But people don't just die for no reason." Sunny insisted.

Which was true there was always a reason. "I know, but for now, let's just worry about a good night sleep, that way we can handle whatever comes our way in the morning, alright?"

Sunny nodded and then curled up next to Amelia squeezing in tight to cuddle. The older girl wrapped her arms around the child and held her tight to her body. The action's comfort both for Sunny and Amelia alike.

"Goodnight kiddo try to sleep well."

Chapter Two - Reality Hits

AS THE SUN BEGAN TO rise for the day outside Anthony and Sam each awake and reviewing what they gathered in the house. The two friends discussed each of their lists compiled yesterday. Sam's food provisions and Anthony's living supplies each took up a page. Individually they searched the house looking for anything close to resembling a weapon or food. With the decision finalized last night, all food would be stored in the kitchen and all weapons in the garage. They didn't want Sunny getting into anything that might hurt her.

Sam went outside to the back yard to assess the safety of the fence. Anthony observed Sam fortifying parts of it. In all probability it was a good idea, who knew what the future held or if anything sinister laid in their future? His dad had sprung for heavy duty wood for the fence about five years ago. It still held up through the hurricanes and was in great condition. After an inspection, the only issue discovered came in the form of parts of the wooden gate needing to be repaired. Sam found the spare two by fours in the garage and taken charge in its repair ensuring all of it functioned properly.

Anthony found six guns in total including; two riffles, one shot gun, and three pistols, or at least what he thought a pistol looked like. Truth be told Amelia should have been doing the assessment for weapons and food, however she still slept. When he looked in on her he saw that Sunny was there, so he assumed the two girls experienced a rough night.

"The three loose posts on the fence are now secure and ready for use. Do you know if there are any locks we might use to install on the fence to ensure people stay out?" Sam asked after he walked into the kitchen and started washing his hands.

"Yeah I believe so, I'll go retrieve some out of the garage my dad has a few locks I think."

Sam washing his hands made Anthony think of something he hadn't before, water. What would happen to their water supply? He had watched his mom pay a monthly bill however the idea where they got it from slipped past his recollection.

"Hey man, if crap hits the fan do you have any idea if water will still flow?" He asked Sam after handing him two locks.

"No clue. Isn't water like a natural thing?"

Anthony moved his shoulders up and down, "No clue."

Sam held up the locks, "What's the code for these, man?"

"Easy, three fifteen four, Amy and my birthday."

Sam rolled his eyes and walked back outside laughing to secure the two gates.

"Morning." Amelia said from behind Anthony.

He turned around and smiled, "Hey sis. How did you sleep? I saw you shared your bed with a visitor."

"She got scared, but we slept alright. Better than I thought I would given what all happened yesterday."

"Good, glad you were okay. I had nightmares all night, I couldn't wipe their images out of my mind. Been up for a while, easier than sleeping."

Amelia walked to her brother and wrapped her arms around him giving him a hug. "I'm sorry Bub."

"Me too Amy. Me to."

After a momentary embrace, Amelia walked away from her brother and went towards the fridge. She looked like she was assessing the situation when her brother chimed in. "Sam went through the food supply already and made note of what we do and don't have."

"Okay," Amelia said, "and what did Sam determine."

"Food won't be an issue for a while."

Amelia shook her head back and forth. "I should be the one doing this, most of our foods are perishables. We need to stock up on canned items, plus we need to get vegetables we can stock pile or can."

"Seriously?" Anthony questioned.

"Yes, don't you remember anything about survival?"

"Some," he shrugged with his shoulders, "I am more suited in physical tasks than homemaker tasks."

"Anthony! This isn't a homemaker task this is survival and I refuse to be offended by you first thing in the morning. I'll make a list and I'll handle food prep for the time being."

The back door opened and both Anthony and Amelia turned around and acknowledged Sam as he enters the kitchen.

"Morning Amelia. Thanks for taking care of Sunny last night."

"No problem Sam, my pleasure." Amelia paused for a moment, "I tried calling Charlotte, and she didn't answer at all. I spoke to Kelly last night, she is staying with Zach. She wasn't able to get ahold of Charlotte either. I don't know what is going on out there but this is scary."

Anthony lowered his head briefly and then looked at his sister, "I think we need to face the reality that life is changing forever. We need to worry about our immediate needs. As much as we love our friends I think the people in this house are who we focus on."

Sam nodded his heads, "Sadly I think you're right."

Amelia let out a sigh and then she turned towards her brother and looked at him head on, "Sunny and I will go handle the food while you and Sam head out to do your stuff. We all need to meet back at the house by noon."

"Amelia you and Sunny are not going out alone." Anthony declared.

"We are, there are food things we need to acquire in order to ensure we don't suffer any immediate issues and you can't handle that."

"I'm not okay with my little cousin roaming around right now alone." Sam interjected.

"She won't be alone she will be with me and if we don't get a head start on some of these things people will wipe everything out. Boys now isn't the time to be babies, we all gotta step up." Mother taught Amelia to stand her ground, she was finally testing out her skill.

Anthony regarded his sister, who thought she was a master of the art of ignoring both men in the room. He figured she had some agenda up her sleeve and didn't want them to interfere with it. "Sam you wanna grab something to eat and then head out?"

"I was thinking of grabbing a banana and string cheese, which will be enough for me."

"Good idea me too, Amy, be safe please. I love you and can't stomach anything happening to you."

Amelia turned her head out from the fridge and then her whole body turned around. She reached out and handed each of them a cheese stick. "I love you guys too, and you all need to be just as careful, okay? Home by noon, no exceptions, anyone. And charge your cell phones!"

"Yes ma'am" the guys said in unison.

Anthony stepped over to his sister and gave her a hug and when he backed away he witnessed Sam do the same thing, except he added a kiss on her cheek. His mind did a double take, Anthony wondered what that was about and was going to ask about it on their way to handle errands today.

"See you two later. Sunny and I will have a nice break from the noise with you two gone."

Anthony rolled his eyes and watched Sam grab the keys to the car they came over in last night. They walked out of the kitchen and then out of the house, grabbing only their jackets in case it rained.

"What's up with you and my sister?" Anthony wasted no time asking as they got into Sam's vehicle.

"Nothing why?"

"Don't try and give me a load of crap I'm not blind!"

"Nothing happened Anthony."

"Uh huh Sam, you better not hurt her I will beat your ass good if you do."

The two didn't say much else for the five-minute drive to Sunny's house. When they pulled into her driveway both boys held their breath.

"Thank God we left her with Amy." Sam said looking at the driveway.

"They must have been driving when it happened." Anthony stated.

Sam lowered his head, Anthony noticed a new sadness coming over his life-long friend. His voice was shaky, but Anthony could make out what he said. "I pray they didn't suffer."

Amelia and Sunny had a quick egg and bacon breakfast before packing up a few essentials. They then piled in her car to head out. She didn't want to risk hearing anything on the radio with Sunny sitting right there next to her, so she pushed her CD button and her mixed disc started to shuffle through songs.

"Where did Sam go?" Sunny's voice came out soft but the worried tone still evident in her voice.

"He and my brother are going see if your folks are okay and if they aren't then they will bring back some of your clothing and toys to our house."

"My parents aren't okay. I know it." She said sadly.

"We don't know yet Sunny, try to stay hopeful." Amelia knew it was a risky deal telling the little girl to have hope, but she just couldn't find it in her to talk about horrible deaths with the child. They all knew no one was alive looking for Sunny, Sam hadn't received any phone calls inquiring, or any replies or answers to his calls or texts. The guys had told her about the burial plans, somehow, Amelia just wanted to pretend a little longer.

"If they are alive they would have called Sam's phone by now. I yelled at him for not keeping me where they thought I was."

The conversation made Amelia's heart break. This little girl knew that her own fate was doomed, and she was sitting here with a practical stranger putting on a brave face. She could learn a lot from Sunny.

"Are you sure you're okay Sunny?" When Amelia looked in her direction she noticed the pools of tears starting to form on her eyes. Seeing the little girl break down after being so strong was too much for Amelia. Without a moment's hesitation she pulled the car over to the side of the road and put it into park.

Sunny looked over at Amelia and after she unbuckled her seat belt she jumped into Amelia's arms. The two clung together tight right there for twenty minutes each crying with one another. Their parents, gone, and there was nothing either of them could do to bring them back to life.

"I'm sorry Sunny, I promise we will help you through this no matter what happens."

"I know Amy, Sam would never leave me with someone he doesn't trust. That much makes me feel better."

Such a smart girl she was, and that made Amelia want to protect her more. As she pulled out of her driveway she looked around at her neighbors' houses. A lot of people had one or two vehicles in their driveways, but no one was outside. Amelia didn't know if it was because everyone seemed to be dead like her parents or if it was because the four of them all acted scared.

When she turned out onto the main drive heading to the grocery store she saw one other car on the road driving. The person behind the wheel was a man and he looked to be older than her. She had a moment of hope when she realized others were alive. Part of her wanted to follow the car because with no one answering at the police department or other family members, she didn't know if she would come across an adult again. However, the little girl next to her insisted on the grocery store, so that was where she drove.

Traveling at a safe speed of forty miles per hour Amelia and Sunny made it to the parking lot of their destination five minutes later. There were plenty of vehicles in the parking lot, but no one was moving. It suddenly occurred to Amelia that they would be walking into a grave yard.

"Sunny, make sure you stay next to me. We don't know what we will find when we go inside."

"Okay Amy." Her soft voice responded with pain in her tone. As Amelia looked over at the child she saw tears forming.

"Honey are you okay?"

"Just scared."

Amelia second that emotion, she was scared too, but they needed to do this to protect their survival.

The two girls parked in front of the store not in a parking place, and walked towards the motion sensor doors. As they approached the doors parted and the girls walked inside. The stench of death wafted through the air and hit Amelia's nose making Amelia reach out for Sunny's hand. Holding each other tightly they grabbed one cart and made their way to the vegetable section. Amelia tried hard not to look at the bodies that were starting to decay along the floors.

Hundreds of bodies began to decompose in the store and Amelia felt her stomach churning with disgust. What would cause all of this? The two tried to just focus on their task at hand. They grabbed ten heads of lettuce then moved to the potato section. Then they grabbed ten ten-pound bags of russet potatoes, six bags of the five pounds of red potatoes, and then they tossed in over twenty of the sweet potatoes. As they approached the corn Sunny tossed in as many ears of corn that laid out on display. Amelia went over to the carrots and cleared out everything she could and as Sunny pushed the cart forward Amelia tossed in tomatoes and peppers until most of the selections were inside their cart.

"I think we are going to need another cart." Amelia said out loud.

"I can go get us one." Sunny offered.

"Okay, but be quick about it." Amelia didn't want the little girl out of her sight for very long.

As she looked around the Publix Grocery store she realized she should also stock up on toiletries. Who knew what they were in store for.

"Here we go!" Sunny was smiling as she pushed the cart over towards Amelia dodging the dead bodies. It was probably the sense of pride she got from helping.

"Take this full cart and go over to the fruit. Pile up anything you can find that you like to eat. Like strawberries, blueberries, bananas, apples, just anything you want."

"I can do that."

Watching her push the heavy cart across the aisle made Amelia feel bad for not helping, but she wanted to keep the girl busy. Now she needed to find easy non-perishable foods. "I'm going over to this aisle, I will be right back."

With a nod from Sunny acknowledging her, she turned towards the cereal aisle and made her way down the rows. After settling on Fruit Loops, Cheerios and Rice Crispy she put all the boxes she could find in the cart and then made her way to the canned food aisle. She tossed in soups, vegetables, pastes, anything she could think of. Sunny came running down the row to find her, she had left the cart where it had been.. "I think we need another cart!" She claimed. After retrieving a third cart, together they walked over to the paper product aisle and put several paper towels and toilet papers into the basket along with trash bags and cleaning products. As they were walking back to pick up the other cart Sunny pulled Amelia's shirt stopping them in front of the candy aisle.

"Can we get some?" Sunny looked innocent as she stared at an M & M display.

"Of course, sweetie." They piled in an assortment of treats and then made their way to the other basket. Since the one Amelia filed up with non-perishables was lightest she had Sunny push that one as they went to their car. After loading everything into brown bags for easy storage they piled the groceries inside the trunk and back seat took some time but once both carts were empty Amelia realized she forgot one important thing. They took the carts back towards the soda aisle where she put a dozen cases of bottled water into two carts and went back to their vehicle. They barely had enough room for all the supplies.

"How long do you think this will keep us?" Sunny asked.

"No clue, but we can come back if we think we need more after we unload all of this stuff."

Amelia took advantage of all of the paper bags around. Once the groceries were handled she grabbed extra stacks of paper bags and tossed them onto the pile of goods.

"What do we need those for?" Sunny asked.

"Never know when we will need help starting a fire and need kindling." Amelia spent many nights with her father camping. She knew how hard it could be to find kindling if you weren't prepared.

The girls drove back to Amelia's house in silence listening to the music that played in the speakers. When they turned into the subdivision Amelia noticed that now there appeared to be some kids in the neighborhood walking around. No adults just kids, exactly like it was at the store, only adults died. Except they didn't see any other children at the store.

"Do you think these kids will want the food we have with us?" Sunny inquired.

Amelia thought about that, she didn't know how long life was going to be rough and she didn't want to share food with all the kids in her neighborhood. "I don't know but I think it would be best if we kept it a secret that we have all of this."

As they pulled into her drive way she opened the garage door with the remote and backed the car into the safety of her house. She made sure the garage door was closed all the way before she got out of her car.

"Why did we do that?" Sunny asked.

"Just to keep us safe kid, always have to be prepared."

"Oh."

The girls assessed the best way to unload and store their food. Amelia decided it would be best to move everything into the kitchen where she could better access how to store the items. It took both of them about an hour of working before the car was emptied and the items were organized. Nothing that they brought home required refrigeration which was what

Amelia had wanted. She opened the pantry and decided the cereal and canned items can easily be stored in there where the rest of their stock had been. It was the vegetables that she worried about. To keep Sunny busy, she had her divide all the toilet paper up by the three bathrooms they occupied and dispersed them accordingly.

Before Amelia knew it, the time had flown by and it was now a quarter to noon and her stomach began growling. She was famished, and she knew the boys were about to be back and they would be hungry too. She looked around the refrigerator to decided what she would be making for lunch.

The two guys slowly walked into Sam's aunts' home. They had seen his aunt and uncle in their vehicle smashed into the garage. The blood from the impact of the vehicle with the brick house was a sight that both boys won't ever forget. Sam's uncle had his nose bashed in and blood was covering his body. His aunt had her eyes wide open staring back at them when they looked in the car. Sam won't be able to explain the image to Sunny, ever.

"Sam come on." Anthony encouraged his friend to continue walking into the house. They didn't spend any time downstairs instead they moved up the one flight of steps and walked into Sunny's room. Here they found one backpack, which Anthony knew would not suffice in depth enough for packing. "I'll go look for a suitcase." He said.

As he walked out of the girl's room he heard his friend start going through items. Sam knew his aunt and uncle would be dead but seeing the image was too much for anyone. Anthony found two more suit cases in the hall closet, he brought them back to the room and set them on the bed.

"How about we fill the backpack with toys and stuffed animals then the two suitcases with clothing."

"Sounds like a good idea." Sam responded with.

The two guys worked silently grabbing clothing from the closet and drawers and placing in the containers. One suitcase held the closet clothing and the other the drawers. Anthony would need to remember to make sure the spare room was cleared out so Sunny had plenty of room for all her items.

The backpack was filled with the toys that appeared to be played with along with all the stuffed animals on her bed. They also grabbed her two pillows and all her blankets that they could find.

"I think as much as we could bring to her that is hers will give her comfort and help her during this." Sam said to Anthony.

"You're right, you should grab a couple of the family pictures maybe even a photo album. That way she can always remember them."

Anthony watched Sam as he walked into the bathroom where he found another bag. He put Sunny's toiletries and hair products into the bag and then shut the door.

"Sam I'm so sorry about your family."

"Nothing we can do, both of us are in the same situation. All we can do is protect the girls."

Anthony nodded his head and walked the suitcases out to the car leaving Sam in the house.

Thirty minutes later, from the front door Anthony asked, "Ready to go?" as he walked back into the house.

Sam walked out of the master bedroom holding a shotgun and pistol in his hand along with two heavy duty knives and what appeared to be an army ranger bag.

"What's all that?" Anthony asked Sam.

"My uncle was in the military, I thought his supplies would come in handy. There is a heavy duty first aid kid on the bed too, can you go grab that along with the supplies of flash lights?"

"Yep will do."

"In the garage there are supplies of water also, we should load those up as well."

"Do you have the keys to your uncle's truck anywhere? We could use the extra space. I think your aunt and uncle will take up most of the room otherwise."

"Good idea." Sam went into his aunt and uncle's bedroom and came out a few minutes later jingling the keys. "Got em."

Anthony nodded at his friend, "Let's load up."

The boys spent some time clearing out the items that they each thought could be useful. The last thing they grabbed before the bodies was a fire pit that was still in the box; Sam had worried about what to do with their trash overflowing in the house with the reality of no garbage men anymore.

Being physically strong had never been Anthony or Sam's forte but today it became more apparent they needed to work out. Lifting the dead bodies and making room for them in the truck bed hadn't been easy. There had been a lot of discussion on where to place them, or if they needed to stack them. It had disturbed both boys immensely and they had wanted to forget about it.

By the time they were heading back to Anthony's house it was eleven thirty and they knew that the girls would be arriving home right at noon. The first morning without parents and they had survived, hopefully their days continued being this easy.

As they pulled into the neighborhood Anthony's cell phone went off and he saw it was his sister calling. "Hey Amy." He sounded happy to talk to his twin.

"Yeah we are about to be there in a minute, go ahead and open it for us and I will pull in. We picked up another vehicle, can you bring ours out to the street? Thanks."

Anthony used his cell phone to call Sam, who picked up after the first ring. "She wants us to unload inside the garage said she saw kids earlier and doesn't want anyone knowing we have supplies."

"Amelia is very smart, you're lucky." Sam said.

"I think you mean we're lucky because we're in this together."

"Together, yeah."

The car backed into the garage and as Sam stepped out of the car he saw Sunny standing there next to Amelia. She had tears in her eyes already before he even said anything. He walked over to her and knelt down on one knee.

"I am so sorry Sunny."

Her tears ran down her cheeks, "Did you bring home Mommy and Daddy?"

Sam nodded his head up and down as he grabbed his cousin in a hug and held her tight.

Amelia and Anthony unloaded the supplies from the car as the other two grieved together.

"I promise I won't let anything happen to you, I love you and I'm not letting you go."

"I love you to Sam, I'm just scared."

"We're all scared Sunny, but at least we still have each other." Sam's words sounded brave, but his face showed that he was equally as scared as his six-year-old cousin.

Their existence altered forever, nothing could go backwards. The four of them, even if they survived, all orphans, only had each other. Tough choices were going to have to be made and it wasn't going to be easy. But they would find a way to survive one way or another. They would just have to take it one day at a time.

That night they had all agreed the tree in the front yard would be their parents last resting place. After the supplies had been unloaded, the guys went to Sam's house and retrieved his mom and dad. Together all four of them dug deep holes, as close to six feet as they could measure. They only made three, husband and wife staying together for all of time.

Sunny cried through the entire process and Amelia almost right along with her. Sam and Anthony had found ways to remain more stoic, but the ordeal left lasting impressions that never would leave their thoughts.

As she hugged her mom and then her dad followed by her aunt and uncle, the dark clouds started to form overhead. She wasn't ashamed to cry

"Now we will have them with us forever." Sunny said.

"That's right sweetie, we will." Amelia's arm draped over Sunny and the two girls stood there, looking at the holes that now were their parents. As they grieved they both knew this wasn't the end, it was only the beginning.

Chapter Three – A Father's Final Gift

AMELIA HAD TAKEN IT upon herself to go through her father's gear. While the two of them were on their hunting trips Amelia and her father discussed the possibilities of the apocalypse. He was one of those dad's where you knew, to him what he was saying made total sense, but to anyone else he sounded insane. The joke was on everyone else now because her dad had been right all along. Inside his hunting gear she had found in the side pocket an 'apocalypse bible' as it was labeled.

When she opened to page one she couldn't believe what she had found. It was a note written from her dad to her and Anthony. She began to read it.

Anthony & Amelia,

If you are reading this letter then I am going to assume that my world has finally come to an end and I am no longer there. Because if you are reading this and I am still alive you will be in trouble! Growing up in my younger life I was a Boy Scout, something I am very proud of. They always instilled in us to be prepared and that's what I hope I had been able to do for each of you by the time this point came. I hope that I passed from this world peacefully and I didn't give cause for you two to worry. I hope that we got to say goodbye. If we didn't then know this one thing. You two are the most important people to your mother and me. We love you beyond words. You both make us proud, and every day you two strive for your best.

In the event that I left this world due to zombies, which you know I have always predicted, I leave to you two my final gift. A survivor's guide. Inside this document you will find a lot of information. Some of it pertains to our house and how to operate everything. Others are how to build certain tools or storage's that you will need in order to make it. For example, eventually the water will shut off. Therefore, I enclosed instructions on how to store an endless water supply. This is of course assuming everything went down in a rainy season month.

I am also leaving instructions on how to work the solar panels of the house and the water heater. I bought an electric one, so you will not need to worry about a gas hook up. You will need to go out and buy deep freezers. You will find emergency money under the mattress in my room, around four thousand dollars. If money is still being used of course. Grab up as much as you can food wise, you can always freeze a lot of items.

Make sure you look through the instructions and familiarize yourself with how the house works. Also, in our bedroom is the gun safe. The code is your birthdates.

Make sure you two take care of each other. If you can reach out to your Uncle Mack or grandfather please do. They both are all you two have left besides each other.

Amelia, you're going to need to teach your brother how to skin animals. I'm sorry that I never got to take you hunting Anthony. I own several books in my room on how to skin and cook wild game that I am sure you will find useful.

Also, your mother wants me to add in here that her kitchen is set-up so her stove can switch from gas to electric. Make sure you switch it away from gas, you don't need to worry about a gas leak in addition to everything else.

Make sure you stock up on batteries. Change out all the smoke alarms and carbon monoxide detectors. In the spare room in the closet you will find first aid survival supplies along with the hurricane preparedness kit. I hope you never have to use them.

My children I love you and you always will be my pride and joy.

I'll keep my eye on you from the other world, I will always be with you.

We love you both now and forever,
Mom & Dad

Amelia wiped away tears as she read the letter. Inside the book as promised she found the instruction manual with details graphed out on how to build lots of different items. It was almost a blue print to building a compound. She never felt so glad her father was eccentric as she did in this exact moment.

She gathered up all of what she just discovered and walked downstairs and into the garage. There she could see Sam and Anthony working diligently on something. She gently placed the items in her arms on the ground and cleared her throat.

"Dad left us a message. An apocalyptic message." She looked at Anthony with tears filled in her eyes, "It includes essentially a step by step guide on what to do to survive. Even how to collect water and make irrigation's."

Anthony took two steps towards her and had her wrapped in his arms. He let her cry the tears she held deep inside. When she got around to showing him the letter she unearthed he cried too. A message from the afterlife.

"Oh Amelia, I am sorry you were alone when you found all this." Anthony continued to hold onto his twin as he read over the message. When he saw the 'mom and dad' scrawled in his father's penmanship he couldn't hold back the emotion.

As the two of them shed tears for their parents Sam stood back quietly observing. Amelia noticed him trying to avoid watching them and she reached her hand out towards him. Beckoning him to join them.

The three of them were becoming more than the family that they had already felt like. After a lifetime of growing up together. These emotions and feelings were different.

"Dad wants us to go get freezers." Amelia said to her brother as she wiped off the tears on her cheeks.

"Why?" Sam questioned.

"For storage of food Sam. We need to read this and do it. Maybe we should go right now and get the freezers." Amelia was reading through the letter again, pointing to Anthony on the spot where their father instructed them to get freezers.

"Any idea where we would pick them up at?" Sam shrugged.

"What about a Home Depot or Lowes type place?" Anthony answered.

"It's a good thing we have the truck now, wonder how many freezers that bed can hold." Amelia said in Sam's direction.

"Only one way to find out. My lady, we will acquire you some freezers." Sam winked at Amelia and then gave a pretend bow in her direction.

"I am going to start cooking something. The manual here explains how to switch the stove from gas to electric. Guess I should probably do that first." Amelia opened the guide to the appropriate page in the manual and began reading. "Hey what exactly is an Allen wrench?"

Sam perked up, "Maybe I should come help you do that. You know, don't want you to hurt yourself."

Amelia looked at him through her tear stained eye lashes. He was smiling at her and she couldn't help returning the gesture. "Thank you Sam."

"For the record, I am not a fan of this at all between you two." Anthony said. His chest seemed to be puffed out for some strange reason and his voice appeared deeper than it had just moments before.

"Fan of what?" Amelia said to her brother innocently.

"You know what I am talking about missy," Anthony wiggled his pointer finger in the direction of his sister. "Sam knows too. And I don't like it." Anthony stormed out of the garage pushing past both of them.

"He really has anger issues." Sam teased, as the two of them moved into the kitchen.

"He takes after our dad, but you knew that. Now again back to this Allen wrench thingy, what does it even look like?" Amelia pointed down towards the instruction manual and put her brother to the back of her mind. She wasn't ready herself yet to talk about what was happening. What had been happening for the past year between her and Sam?

SUNNY HAD MASTERED being silent and not seen a long time ago. She sat in the corner of the hallway as the three of them all discussed Amelia and Anthony's dad's letter. She missed her own mom and dad too but no one was talking about them. Not even Sam, who knew them. She had spent her free hours crying, because what else was she supposed to do? The rain had come and gone, just like her tears, falling in different waves. Somehow she found comfort in the sound of the water beating against the roof of the house. It almost seemed healing to her.

She made her way back to her bedroom. Amelia instructed her to call it her room that way she would get used to the idea. Her cousin brought over a lot of items she loved, stuff she actually played with. It had taken a couple hours to unpack everything Anthony and Sam retrieved from her own house .Now that everything had its own place, she felt good. Sunny wasn't a big fan of clutter, in fact she couldn't function in it. While she was cleaning out one of the drawers in her new room she found Anthony's baby album. Tiny little fingers and toes.

Sunny hated knowing she would never get to have her photos like this. Yes, Sam had brought her some albums but it wasn't the same. Amelia and Anthony grew up in this house and here Sam and Sunny were just latching on for the ride to enjoy this house. It wasn't really theirs. She wouldn't have any more photos of her life and what was going on.

Her state of depression became something she could easily slip into if she wasn't careful. She hated the depression. She tried to focus on the good, but all that came out happened to be more tears. Once again she noticed that the rain accompanied her cries. The whole earth around her wept alongside her.

It wouldn't take the others long to realize what Sunny was realizing. Her emotions controlled the weather and if she wasn't careful he could wipe out everyone with a flood.

There was a soft knock on the door and Anthony pushed open her room door. He smiled at her but she could tell he was up to something. "Hey Sunny."

"Hiya Sam."

"You hungry? Amelia is making some good soup she concocted."

"I'm okay for now, thanks Anthony." Sunny didn't want to go downstairs. It wasn't that she didn't like Anthony, it was that she didn't feel comfortable asking him for assistance just yet.

"You need to eat Sunny, come on, this will help your strength. Get on down here."

She obliged with no argument. She didn't want to cause too big of a scene. There were going to be a lot more days ahead, days she knew that would be bad. She may as well leave the arguments for those days and not for today.

"Hey Amelia, it smells great." She said as she strode in with confidence into the kitchen.

"Hope your hungry everyone I made enough to feed an army." Amelia replied.

"I'm starving, let's eat!" Sam declared from his newly acquired spot at the table.

"Hold your horses there cowboy, young ladies get to cut in line." Amelia guided Sunny across the room. Who promptly looked over her shoulder and stuck her tongue out at her older cousin in a teasing form.

Sunny thought to herself, *maybe all of this will work out after all.*

AFTER DINNER ANTHONY and Sam made their first run to Home Depot. They were able to load two deep freezes into the truck bed without causing a major issue. The next morning Amelia and Anthony took off to the meat market where they ended up spending six hours of their day going through meat to determine if it was savable or not. Sam and Anthony were arguing over where to store the freezers when Amelia walked into the room. She didn't want to deal with all of the craziness that they were trying to do with said freezers. She asked them to bring them into the den and to stop complaining. Lucky for the two of them, that was exactly what they decided to do.

"Amelia, now you can go obtain as much meat as your little heart desires." Sam said to her.

"Yeah I can, thanks to you." She grinned over at him.

"Knock it off you two, man you're gonna make me puke." Anthony stormed out of the room after he had finished assembling his parts of the freezer.

The two of them laughed at Amelia's brother, they knew it was going to get worse before it was going to get better.

"Will you go shopping with me tomorrow Sam?" She asked.

"Of course I will. What's on the menu?"

"Meat, lots and lots of meat." She grinned at him.

"Maybe we need a third freezer, can you freeze vegetables?" He asked her.

With a shrug of her shoulder she stated, "I don't see why not, I mean they have frozen peas at the store, right?"

"Yeah, true they do. Hey do you want to maybe help me with something?" Sam asked, his tone a bit off.

"Okay? What is it?"

"I think I need to try and find some of my other cousins. Sunny wasn't the only one who is younger and I've called the houses, no one answered."

"Oh, yeah. Okay sure, I can help you. Not sure what you would want me instead of Anthony for though."

Sam smiled, "Well, you're a girl and they are literally all girl cousins. One of my aunts had four girls. I think one is a little older than our age and the other are younger than fifteen. Not sure. Thought maybe we could bring them here."

"In this house?" Amelia asked with a gasp.

He shook his head back and forth, "No not in this house but what about the neighbor's house? Sam told me the couple next door was old. Thought if we found my cousins we could bring them back and I could help them clean out the house next door. Maybe it would help Sunny too."

"They were related to her as well?"

"No, she's from my dad's side, but my Aunt Frieda's kids some are near her age."

"Oh that makes sense. Okay, when would you want to go looking?" Amelia had finished her examination of the freezers and now started working on packing the vegetables in the brown bags she retrieved from the store. After sorting them she began putting them in crates. Eventually Sam knelt down and joined her in this tedious chore.

"I'd like to go today. If that's okay. It's been a couple days and I don't know if they are okay. I'm worried."

"Sure Sam. We can go. I'm done with this stuff now, let's tell Anthony where we are off too."

"Thank you for understanding." Sam leaned over and kissed her cheek lightly pressing his lips against her skin.

Amelia's face flushed and she smiled a little larger this time. "My pleasure."

The two of them walked out of the den and saw Sunny and Anthony playing cards in the living room. Sam told them what his plans were and at first Anthony wasn't okay with letting his sister take the lead on this. He wanted to be the one out there with his friend, but he could see she was gun-ho set on making this quest with Sam, so Anthony didn't push the issue.

"Maybe why you two are gone I can start cleaning the house next door. Sunny could help." Anthony said, looking at Sunny for confirmation.

"Sure." She shrugged, the little girl in her showing more and more today.

"Thanks you guys, we will call once we get to my cousin's. See you soon."

Sam and Amelia took his uncle's truck, they backed out of the driveway and left the neighborhood. More kids were starting to show up around the streets, they noticed as they drove across Saint Pete. Amelia had made the mistake of looking into a couple of the stalled cars on the road, the dead bodies beginning to rot made her stomach churn on sight.

"You can't think about it." Sam said in a stoic tone.

"About what?" She replied.

"The death, you just can't think about it. You have to put it to the back of your mind."

"How can you do that when it is literally all around us? Everywhere we look there is either lost kids, lost teens or dead adults."

"I know but Amelia, we don't know what is happening and we certainly do not know if there will be anything else coming up. You can't focus on the death. You have just got to think about the future and the positive. My dad always told me, if you focus on the good than bad will stay away."

"Well we know that didn't exactly work out well for your dad now did it?" Amelia retorted, her tone angrier than she intended.

"Fair enough. But I don't see how focusing on death will help anyone."

The two didn't say another word for the rest of the drive. When Sam pulled into the house that his aunt owned he noticed that there were no lights on. It didn't seem like anyone was home.

Amelia looked up at the house through the windshield and made the observation, "Something's happened here, you can see the windows are broken." She pointed her right arm up and extended her hand to where her right pointer finger aimed at the front window on both the first and second floors. "I should have brought Daddy's gun."

"I did grab a gun, but I don't want to have to use it. I hope they are okay." Sam's voice was panicked.

Sam jumped out of the truck and motioned with his hands for Amelia to stay in her seat. He moved around the side of the house in a stealth mode, something he learned off playing video games. He had the gun pointed up in the air and was tip toeing around to the front door when he heard.

"You don't even know what you're doing holding the gun like that, here give it to me." Amelia's curt tone scared Sam. He jumped straight up in the air and then grabbed his chest.

"What the hell Amy I told you to stay in the truck."

"When have you known me to listen, now give me the pistol?"

"No, now quiet."

She shrugged her shoulders and the two of them proceeded to explore the house. There had been obvious signs of a fight. The furniture was turned over and items were thrown around the house. The smell that permeated the air let them know there was for sure at least one dead body.

It was when they entered the kitchen that the found the source of the stench. "Oh my god." Sam said. "It's Aunt Frieda and her daughter Cassie. She was the one I told you was a little older than us."

"How much older Sam?" Amelia asked.

He shrugged, "I don't know maybe like nineteen, twenty max."

"So an adult, weird." Amelia looked around, "Where are the other ones, your younger cousins?"

"I don't know?" Sam started calling out for them but after a full search of the house it was clear they were nowhere to be found.

"I'm sorry Sam, I know you were wanting to find them." Amelia put her arm around him to try and offer some comfort.

"I just don't know where they would have gone. I mean they are kinda young to be on their own." Sam had moved to the couch and put a cushion back on to sit down.

"Do you want to leave them a note, maybe they will come back?" Amelia took the seat beside him.

"Yes, but first I need to burry my aunt and cousin. I wonder where my uncle is, he must not have been home when this all happened." Sam wiped tears from his eyes and then left the couch and went out to the garage. He returned with two shovels in hands and one set of work gloves. "I brought you some gloves that way you don't get blisters."

Amelia took the gloves without comment as they moved to the back yard and began to dig one large hole.

ANTHONY AND SUNNY HAD spent the better part of the afternoon cleaning the house next door. They removed all the items that they thought would be useful to store in the den that Amelia had started. Sunny was grateful that Anthony took it upon himself to remove the elderly couple from their home. She didn't want to be a part of that process at all. While going through the kitchen she discovered a honey trove of candles. She grabbed as many as she could and raced home to store them in her bedroom. Something told her she was going to need it.

As she left her room she heard a cell phone going off in Amelia's room. She walked inside to see the iPhone that Amelia used was sitting on her bed. It was now ringing. She walked across the room and picked up the device and slid the call to accept.

"Hello?"

"Amelia, arc you okay?" A frantic woman's voice said on the other line.

"No I'm sorry she isn't home right now may I take a message?"

"Yeah can you tell her Susie called? Where is she?"

"She's just not here right now and yeah I will tell her you called thanks." Sunny hung the phone up without giving the voice on the other end a second thought. She didn't like the idea of more people joining their group even if they were Sam's family, let alone friends of Amelia's from school. That would just make the place more crowded.

With no second consideration given she erased the memory of answering the phone and went back to work over at the neighbors' with Anthony.

Chapter Four - The New Reality

A LITTLE OVER A MONTH passed since the four formed a new family. They seemed to settle into a grove that worked for all of them. Amelia maintained the house, whether it involved the cleaning or food issues she ran the home. Sunny followed Amelia like a puppy all over the house, and Amelia didn't seem to mind. She taught Sunny simple tasks to follow that would help everyone out, but keep her out of trouble too.

The house itself became a fortress thanks to the upgrades Sam constructed. The windows on the first floor now had boards on them to keep people in the front yard from being able to penetrate into them. Sam believed that the risk of the other teenagers looting homes inside the neighborhood could increase as time went on. They didn't want to give any opportunity for that to happen at their house. He and Anthony took trips to the hardware store and obtained enough ply wood to build a boat with. He boarded up the front side of the window and the inside portion. The double layer made everyone feel more secure.

Sometime into the second week their house lost power. The solar panels that Anthony and Amelia's father installed worked for the most time but with the cloud coverage they weren't able to store enough energy with the panels. This gave them only enough power to run the house at night.

Anthony made the argument that since everyone pilfered items from one store or the other they might as well find a heavy duty solar generator. They managed to find a solar generator at Costco that was large enough to run a house. Their project for the last two days became installing and hooking that generator up to the house's main circuit. Luckily, the circuit to the house was inside of the fenced area so that made everyone more comfortable with it not being stolen.

The appearance that the adults all vanished intensified as days passed and their paths never crossed any other adults, aside from the one Amelia saw driving that first day. The internet seemed to still be up and running. Sam and Anthony searched on YouTube how to install the solar panels and connect the generator. Amelia worried the house would burn down, but the boys assured her it would be okay.

"Ready to flip the switch" Anthony called out as Sam finished the last wiring issue. Amelia and Sunny stood back a few feet in the designated safe zone watching their guys work.

The suspense of the moment left everyone with overwhelming dread. They heard Anthony giving a backwards three count to Sam and as the number one was hit all of them held their breaths as they watched the house light up with energy. It worked and now they possessed one less worry. With power restored it gave their group another victory in the win column.

"It worked!" Sunny yelled as she ran up to her cousin and wrapped her tiny arms around his neck.

All four of them were glad and celebrating. A small victory in the long run, but in so many ways it was their first steps to survival.

Amelia felt it best to kill two birds with one stone, so while they had their mission of confiscating the generator Amelia also asked them grab two window AC units. She'd been working all week to finish converting the downstairs den into a food storage room and needed to find a way to get the room to stay between forty and sixty degrees, while maintaining normal temperature in the rest of the house. Her and Anthony went out and found barrels and storage containers that way all their food could last as long as possible.

Sam had come up with the idea that instead of organizing everything by type organize by date acquired that way they could eat the oldest items first. Everyone was contributing to the success.

Sunny was in charge of laundry which she loved. The group had decided that they did not want to run the washer and dryer because of the amount of resources that would require. They went back to Sunny's home and retrieved her kiddie pool from the garage. They set something up in the back yard with clothes hangers and a make shift wash board. Every morning Sunny took the clothes from the day before out to the back yard and washed them by hand and hung them to dry and by dinner time she was able to fold them up and bring them in.

The four of them really had found a way to make it all work.

"I think we should find a way to extend our fence." Sam said at dinner that night.

"Extend what way?" Anthony asked.

"To cover the front yard too, that way the girls can get out of the house more and feel safe."

"I think we get out just fine." Amelia declared.

"Yeah!" Sunny chimed in.

"Okay, okay, I just wanted to make sure you two were safe."

"I don't think it is worth arguing with both of them, Sam." Anthony laughed as he consumed another bite of the soup his sister had made.

The girls had ventured back to the Publix Grocery store every day that week collecting more items to stock pile. Upstairs each person maintained their own room. Inside each room was a stock pile of toiletries and toilet paper for each person along with extra socks and shoes. They grabbed items in future sizes for each person too, that way when they grew out of something they replaced the item. Anthony insisted on that.

The teenagers worried about their water supply vanishing one day. Sam always wanted to be an engineer. He said he was going to attempt to make the collection and filtration unit for the back yard, for when it rained, based on the survival guide Anthony's dad provided, but that was a project for next week. In the mean time, they collected cases of water. Each bedroom held two cases stored in there along with a box of canned goods in the event of an emergency.

Amelia claimed she came up with a lot of her ideas from *The Walking Dead*, but Anthony said it was because she was always the overzealous one of the two of them. Especially since she had been reading her father's survival books every night before bedtime. She claimed it gave literal step by step instructions on how to live through anything.

"I have something to talk about." Anthony stated as they were finishing dinner.

"What's up?" Sam asked.

"Has anyone noticed that it's only other teens or young kids we see around?" Everyone nodded their head as Anthony continued. "It makes me think that the adults must have been targeted on a mass scale."

"What are you thinking, some kind of new age weapons of mass destruction?" Amelia asked.

"I'm not sure but there has to be a cause."

"Anthony is right, something caused a whole slew of people to just up and die."

"If it was a WMD then wouldn't some government have invaded us by now? I mean we live right near the coast." Amelia protested.

"Amelia has a point," Sam said looking at her and smiling.

"I didn't say I thought it was some mass weapon, I just think something killed on a mass scale." Anthony interjected.

"Why did we live?" Sunny inquired.

The other three in the room remained silent. No one knew the answer to the one question everyone wanted to ask this whole time. Why had they lived?

"I don't think we will ever know what happened." Anthony said. "But that doesn't mean I don't want to try and find out. I would like to go out and look for some sorts of clues."

"By yourself?" Amelia objected.

"No, all four of us, I think we should stay together and not separate."

"I don't know how I feel about that." Sam declared looking down at his cousin. "Sunny is so young."

"Not that young." She retaliated.

"Yes, that young." Sam said more forceful.

"Well the thing is I don't think that anyone should be alone right now, and if we go out looking for answers we should all go together."

"We can talk about this later." Sam sternly said.

They finished their dinner in silence with a lot of tension. Amelia knew her brother wouldn't let this go and she did understand it. She needed to know why her parents died too, she just wasn't sure if she wanted to venture out past their small neighborhood to find out.

Sam sat on the edge of his bed looking around the room at his items he managed to bring over from his home. Parts of his old life were still evident. He had the most treasured of his possessions, but he also had items of his parents. Sam and his father wore almost the same size clothing, and he took most of his dad's clothing. Sam also loved how his mother smelled so he brought over her perfume, just to take a sniff occasionally. At the last visit to his home he saw the family bible, he hesitated when looking at it. Anthony was right, something killed all the adults or at least most of them in this world. That wasn't godly something that could kill on that massive level. He decided to bring it anyway, if nothing else it did contain the family lineage.

"Knock knock," Amelia said from his doorway.

"You can come in." He smiled as he spoke and quickly put down the photograph he was holding.

"I didn't mean to disturb you, but I wanted to talk to you about something." Amelia paced around his room and after a few seconds he motioned for her to take a seat on his bed.

"What's up Amy?"

"You see, eventually the water is going to stop, you know that, right?"

He indicated agreement with his head moving up and down, "I do, that's why we have different water catches around the back yard, so we won't be SOL."

Amelia was moving her head up and down but not saying anything else.

"Something tells me you want to expand on this." Sam grinned as he spoke to her. She really was the prettiest girl they had in school.

"I do, see, I was thinking."

Sam interrupted her, "Careful now, if Anthony hears that you were thinking he may put a thinking gag on you."

"Quiet you," she smirked and leaned into his shoulder. "As I was saying. I've been thinking, we should find a way to have an irrigation system rigged so we can get water into the house without having to go outside. Maybe have it pool into a location in the kitchen or something, so we can stay in the protection of the house because what happens when hurricane weather hits."

"We will have plenty of water then Amy."

She shook her head back and forth, "No we won't Sam. That hurricane weather will not only contaminate our current water supply, but it will over saturate everything with more of a salt water-based liquid which isn't good for us to drink. You know how much water we will lose? And this isn't like the old days where we will get a warning from the news that a hurricane is on the way."

"I hadn't thought about that." Sam sat there silently pondering what Amelia had just told him. He was up for the challenge but didn't know how to execute a solution just yet. "When is hurricane season?"

"June to November I think." She said.

"So, we have a couple months to plan then." He retorted. "Good I will figure up a solution don't you worry."

"I'm not too too worried, I know you will figure something out."

The two sat on the edge of his bed in silence for two minutes. The tension between them had grown over the week. It wasn't a bad tension but a noticeable one.

"Guess I should leave you for the night then."

"You don't have to Amy." He extended his hand out to cover hers, "If you want to stay you can."

"I promised Anthony I would play a game or two of cards with him tonight, I should really get going to that."

"I am sure he would understand if you wanted to," Sam paused a moment and then leaned over and kissed her lips lightly. "Stay."

Amelia's face went from a warm and welcoming look to a scared and anxious one the moment his lips touched hers. That made him feel like a complete fool. He pulled away quickly and immediately started to apologize.

"Amy I'm sorry I thought you and I were on the same page."

She stood up quickly and pretended to smooth her pants out with her hands, "It's fine, and we are. I am sorry, I didn't mean to react like that, I have to go Sam, goodnight."

Before any other words could be exchanged she was out of the room and racing down the hallway. Man, he had blown that. Not just their first kiss, but his first kiss ever. And the girl was found running out of the room and not for a good reason.

Sunny watched from across the hall as her cousin and now new sister kissed. She didn't understand why Sam did that, and it upset her. Upset both the girls it seemed. She knew that they hadn't seen her watching. Sunny knew how to be invisible, that was one thing little kids did well. Overhearing them discuss the water supply worried her too. She had heard Amelia mumbling to herself a few times about preparing for the future. Maybe that's what she was talking about.

She slowly and quietly shut the door to the room she was in, so Sam wouldn't find out she spied. Her room location ended up near Amelia's and that was at the other end of the house. She knew that the room she currently was in would be off limits. But she just wanted to see them. Anthony and Amelia's parents were no longer sitting in the closet but had been buried with the rest of the parents. However, Sunny felt like she could still feel their presence in the room.

The little girl desperately tried to feel her mother's presence and thought maybe if she went where Amelia's mother had died maybe she would feel her own.

"I miss you momma." She said in the tiniest of voices. They had taught her to believe in God and the angels, she hoped they had both become angels when their death came. When she closed her eyes, she could picture their family times together, sitting at the park, laughing or swimming at the community pool.

Sunny became so engulfed in her memories of her past that she hadn't realized Sam came into the room. He had opened the door behind her and had been watching her talk to her dead mother. Her face turned red and she instantly felt embarrassed. She knew she was the youngest by far in her new family, but she didn't want them to see her as a baby, and now Sam would because she was acting like one.

Her face started to crunch up and tears slowly leaked through her now closed eye lids. She was looking at blackness and feeling shame and sadness wash all over her. She knew that Sam had his arms around her and was trying to comfort her, but it wasn't helping. She felt like a storm inside, full of anger and rage. When she had entered this room, it was intended to help her heal, but like the weather outside, the longer she stayed the worse the feelings became.

She swore the more she cried inside the worse the storm became and that suited her just fine. She couldn't hold it in any longer. She missed her parents and needed to let it out.

"Sunny it's okay, you're not alone, we all feel the way you do." Sam said softly in her ear.

"No, you don't, you all feel normal sadness. There is something wrong with me. What I feel isn't normal."

Sam cooed at his cousin and tried to calm her down, "What is it you feel Sunny?"

"Darkness, I feel darkness."

Chapter Five - Things Change

SUNNY LET SAM HOLD her for a while longer before she left his embrace and returned to her own bedroom. Sunny knew Sam was following her to the other bedroom. She had decisions to make and she didn't know how to make them. At the age of six she had already lost her whole family and the life she had known. How does she handle that?

Making matters worse it seemed like every time Sunny cried it would rain outside. She had tried using the iPad she had to search up activities like that, emotions causing rainstorms, but the internet had finally stopped working, it was pointless. Sunny's world felt like not only was it changing daily, sometimes for the better, but ultimately for the worst. She was aware that no matter what was done today, tomorrow would be a new fight and a new life-threatening situation.

"I need to go" she said softly to her cousin Sam. In the background she could hear the thunder from outside. It hadn't been raining today, it seemed out of place to suddenly hear it.

"What caused you to come in here kiddo?"

His voice was calm and cool; she was able to find comfort listening to the tenor of his dialog.

"I saw you kiss Amelia and it bothered me." Another sound of thunder echoed the room, this time it sounded closer.

"Oh," Sam said. Sunny watched him look over her expectantly for a few minutes and then stood up and moved to sit on the bed of his best friends' dead parents. "Did that upset you Sunny?"

She nodded her head and then curled her legs up against her while on the floor. "Yeah I don't want to have to leave."

"Why would we need to leave?" Sam asked with an over exacerbation.

"Because I saw her get angry with you, and they will make us leave."

Sunny had always been smart for her age, but even with her advanced skill set she wasn't quite aware of how things worked with older individuals and relationships. It scared her not understanding and not knowing what the future held for them.

"I promise you," Sam said to her as he held her close, "they aren't kicking us out. Amy and I, we go back and forth. We both really like each other but we are friends and that makes it hard."

"And you're sure she won't make us leave?" Sunny said sniffling her nose and wiping it on her shirt sleeve.

"Yes, I can promise you that for sure."

Sunny nodded and then moved away from her cousin. "I guess then I will go do the rest of my chores." Then just like that she had left the room. When she walked away from Sam, she had heard the rain lightly pelting the roof of the house. Her emotions started to take over and she knew she was losing control. She noticed that as her anger rose the intensity of the storm increased. The weather outside became a full-on calamity now and somehow that made her feel worse.

She wasn't sure if what Sam told her is the truth. He couldn't know for certain she would always get to stay here, but she would choose to have faith in him and in this decision he made. She possessed no other choice anyway.

What happened upstairs through Amelia off kilter badly, she had promised Anthony that nothing would happen between her and Sam, even though she knew she wanted more. It was clear he wanted more with her. She had blown it, blown their first kiss along with her first kiss ever. She made a mess and now she was going to cook him dinner like nothing went wrong. How was she going to even focus? Anthony had been on his latest kick about fortification of the house's enhancements. He spent more and more time in the attic doing god knew what, but that wasn't her concern right now.

Every night she took inventory of the food and checked each item for spoiling. As of her latest count they were doing good holding steady on their vegetables. Their meat supply was going to run out soon based on their current consumption habits. Which meant they either needed to find more frozen meats or more vegetables that held a good source of protein. Amelia supposed they could always take up hunting their protein down too.

Her mother had made her attend cooking classes, and since their deaths, Amelia was very grateful of it. At least she knew how to balance a meal and cook more than just the basic items. Her only real struggle was seeing how they were going to be able to plan for a real future, one that wasn't just tomorrow or next week but for the next year or ten years.

Before the event happened Anthony, Sam and Amelia were all slated to pick out their colleges this school year, their senior year. Now that exciting future had suddenly been canceled. Each night Amelia sat out on the patio in the front yard watching the neighbors. Kids, children, young teens. None of them seemed to have it together and more and more kids seemed to vanish as days went by. She wasn't sure if it was because they were dying with no food or if they were migrating to some other location. Part of her felt guilty that they hadn't offered their home to the children. She knew realistically that keeping the four of them safe was going to be enough of a challenge. They couldn't take on their whole neighborhood.

Amelia felt deep inside that she should have followed the one adult she spotted on the first day of the event. It was possible he could have helped their situation somehow.

Amelia was now busy in the kitchen putting together a steak stew when Sam walked into the doorway. His frame wasn't big, he was a medium size guy, but he came across large compared to what he had been just six months ago. She stopped mixing at the stove and glanced over to him. She couldn't help smiling.

"I am glad to see you using that." He pointed his finger towards the stove.

Sam had designed a wood burning stove to replace the current stove that had been in the kitchen. Amelia was also worried about the stove taking up too much electricity on the solar panels. None of them were looking forward to the hot showers becoming cold. But they all knew it was a very real possibility that could happen one day.

"I do love the stove Sam. I believe I've told you that before."
She was still gazing over at him with the smile plastered on her
lips. Her gratitude was genuine, and she didn't know how else
to express it.

"I know you did, doesn't mean I don't love hearing it." Sam
smiled at her.

Amelia placed her ladle down on the stovetop and stepped
away from it for a moment; she looked at Sam with earnest
and reverence. She did admire him, and she cared about him. If
Amelia let herself admit the truth, she loved him. She had for a
while now.

"I am a total klutz and I am sorry." Amelia's declaration
took Sam by surprise, which was evident in his reaction.

Sam's facial response at first looked confused, but he quickly caught onto her meaning. "You have nothing to be sorry
about Amy, I'm the one who can't keep my act together."

"But you were so sweet, and I ruined it." Her voice was soft
almost tearful, the remorse evident in the words she quietly
said.

Sam shook his head back and forth, "You didn't ruin anything. Although I have to warn you, Sunny saw it."

"She did?" Amelia said in shocked tone.

"Yes, and she is now afraid you're going to kick us out for
putting the moves on you and you being offended."

Amelia whispered, "I wasn't offended." Her fingers moved
to rest on his arm.

"I hope not." He said softly back.

"Maybe we could try again later, when I am not caught so
much off guard?" Her eyes were looking up at him, her eyelids
batting slowly at him, trying to keep back tears.

Sam let a smile creep slowly onto his face as he placed one hand on the small of her back and pulled her towards him, "I think I like you off guard." His warm lips hit hers a second later and this time instead of protesting she joined in.

Amelia wrapped her arms around his neck and let him kiss her good and hard. By the time they broke apart she could smell the beef starting to burn and pushed out of his embrace and ran to the stove.

"I liked that Amy." He said.

She didn't respond right away, she let the ladle make its way around the soup a few times before determining what to respond with. "Maybe we can have round two tonight, maybe out on a walk?"

"Like a date?" Sam said anxiously.

"Yes, like a date!" Amelia giggled in response.

She nodded her head up and down in agreement to the date, but instead of five thirty like he suggested she said seven. They would meet out at the opening of the fence and travel into the local surroundings tonight to see what the world had to bestow on them.

"Your brother is going to hate this, you know that right?"

She nodded. "I know but we will be eighteen in a couple months and seeing as all the adults we know are gone, I think I can kinda do what I want."

"I like the way you think Amelia."

Amelia grinned at Sam, "Me to." She moved her hand softly on his chest and pushed him back, "Now please let me finish dinner, I'll see you later."

When she went back to focusing on her food preparation she started to feel a little light headed. She knew it was anticipation and excitement. She had always been intimidated by the opposite sex but this time she wasn't going to let fear win. This time she would take charge.

The sun set early that night, around seven fifteen. They had just made it outside of the perimeter of the house as the sky shifted coloring into the reds and oranges that now painted the sky line.

"It's beautiful isn't it?" Amelia said to Sam.

"Yes, it gives off this very peaceful yet surreal vibe when you look out on it."

Sam offered his arm to Amelia and she took it gladly. They walked arm in arm around the first block inside their little world. "I am kind of surprised we haven't spent more time getting to know the people in our neighborhood." He commented.

"Anthony is very worried that people will try and take our supplies."

"I know that, I was just thinking that since we don't know what has happened out here that killed only the adult's maybe it would make more sense if we sort of banned together." Sam was lightly touching her skin on the top of her hand while they walked, caressing it softly with his fingertips.

"How do we know that this is only happening here in Saint Pete?" She asked.

Sam shook his head, "We don't we can only assume."

Amelia snickered, "You know what they say about assuming right?"

They both laughed, and as they turned around the next corner they heard a loud sound, like a bomb going off. They stopped moving and both tensed up, essentially freezing in place.

Amelia stuttered out, "What was that?"

"Some kind of explosion." Sam turned his head looking around.

"There. I see it, smoke!" Amelia said with excitement pointing off in the distance.

"Do you think it was a bomb?" Sam questioned.

"How should I know, I would think if we were under attacked there would be more than one explosion though?"

Amelia's face paled as a thought entered her head. "Sam, you remember when you worried about the natural gas?"

He nodded his head.

"The facility CFG is out that way."

"Who is CFG?" Sam said with a quizzical look on his face.

"Come on you know, Central Florida Gas!" Amelia said with excitement and fright in her voice.

They both turned toward their home and started running. While they were in motion back to the house, Amelia yelled out "Go turn off the gas valve, first thing we have to do is cut the gas to the house!"

As the two ran to their house they could hear other explosions off in the distance starting.

The two made it back onto their property and inside the house. Amelia started running through the place looking for Sunny and Anthony. Sam ran into the garage and found the wrench hanging on the wall. He rushed to the front yard where he started frantically turning the valve into the off position. Once he had successfully cut the flow of gas to their home he fell back into the grass and looked up to the sky. The cloud coverage was back, it looked like rain was about to start back up. It had now rained for a week straight and he didn't know if that was a blessing or a curse.

"Sam did you get it?" Anthony screamed, as he bolted out of the front door and over to the gas main.

"Yeah I did, but man that was scary!"

"Thank god you organized all the tools like that, who knows how long it would have taken to find the right wrench otherwise." Anthony said to his friend. He extended a hand towards Sam who was now moving to stand up.

"We should have done that the day we decided to have a plan in place to keep cooking."

Amelia and Sunny walked outside and came to stand behind the guys. "Cooking is fine but what about showers?" Sunny asked.

"Don't worry Sunny. We have an electric water heater for showers that my dad installed. He was very prepared." Anthony said.

"Do you think we need to cut the gas off to anything else?" Sam inquired.

Shaking his head back and forth, "Nope, it's just this one spot. Hey Sam, how is the irrigation system working?"

"I need to go to the library and look up some books on it," Sam said in a tone that almost sounded like he was embarrassed.

"How are you going to find the book you need?" Sunny asked.

"What do you mean?" Anthony replied.

"If they have no power how will you find it? You can't use the computer anymore."

The three older kids all laughed and looked at one another. They were all thinking back to their librarian Mrs. Potner and how she made them learn the Dewy Decimal System last year.

"Sunny don't you worry I got that covered." Sam smiled at his cousin and said proudly.

"Okay good because I don't want a waterless shower, I need to be clean!" The young girl said with a matter of fact tone.

"You and me sister, you and me both." Amelia placed her arm around Sunny and started to walk back into the house.

Once the girls shut the front door Anthony looked at Sam.

"What were you two doing out here anyway?" He demanded from his best friend.

"We were going for a walk." Sam stated.

"Just a walk?" Anthony inquired.

"Is that really any of your business Anthony?" Sam retorted.

"When it involved my sister, yeah, it kinda is." His tone growing sharper.

Sam shook his head back and forth, "She has a mind of her own, she can make her own choices, you know."

"I am not going to like this am I?" Anthony declared.

Sam looked at his best friend, who was like a brother to him. He couldn't deny what was happening, but at the same time he didn't want to hurt Anthony.

"Not really, but I won't hurt her I promise."

"You can't promise me that." Anthony rebutted.

"Okay I promise you this; I won't intentionally do anything to hurt her, how's that?"

Anthony shrugged, "Better I guess."

"She and I have been building up to this for a while now Anthony. I care for her a lot."

Anthony nodded at his friend. That was all he could do.

When the two guys turned to head back into the house the chain of events that followed would haunt them longer than the dead bodies they had seen. One by one house after house in the area started to explode. Debris and fire was falling all around them. They raced inside and shut the door. The girls came running back into the living room eyes wide open.

"Let's go upstairs and watch." Sunny said, right before she ran up the stairs.

The three of them followed the young six-year-old as she opened her window in her room and they watched as most of their neighborhood went up in smoke.

Sunny had her eyes glued to the series of houses that took turns exploding. It started out in the direction of the original explosion. Amelia pictured the gas lines traveling underground and as they diverted off to each area explosions occurred.

"Guys, we need to turn the gas off to the houses next to us. We don't want our house to accidentally catch on fire." She said.

Sam and Anthony looked at each other and nodded.

"On it," Sam said.

Anthony quickly replied with "Girls you stay here we only have two wrenches anyway, we're going to shut the gas off."

All Amelia and Sunny could do was agree as their men raced out of the house and out into danger. No one knew when their subdivision would start to explode. Amelia held Sunny's hand as the two of them watched Sam and Anthony racing around at the different gas mains.

From the second floor Amelia noticed that some of the other neighborhood children were coming outside to watch the explosion. She noticed Sam talking to some of them and pointing. Anthony was on the other side of the street yelling commands. From her estimate it didn't appear there were too many older teenagers around. Possibly five outside of the three of them. She had a feeling that this would be the event that moved them into taking more people into their home.

"Amelia?" Sunny's voice sounded shaky, and that broke Amelia's heart.

"Yeah sweetie."

"I can help the fire from the explosions by not letting it get any worse."

Amelia didn't know what to say so she just didn't. She held the child closer as the sky turned black and rain started to pour from it.

Sunny clung to Amelia and didn't let go as she cried, the rain intensified as each drop on her cheek ran down her face. Amelia couldn't deny what she was witnessing, but she also couldn't explain it.

Chapter Six - And Then There Were More...

SUNNY STAYED IN BED for the following three days after the CFG explosion. Her body needed the rest. No one talked yet about what had happened with the rainstorm that spurred after the explosion. Sam and Anthony had managed to save twenty or so other houses in their neighborhood from taking off in smoke. All the houses that surrounded their property and the others on their same street. Anthony had been meticulous over the last two days going to each house and taking inventory. Whether it was how many survivors were living there or how much in way of resources they could find in each house. He now had a log and had become the assumed leader of their area.

Sam had taken it upon himself to declare it a war zone. He wasn't still convinced that there wasn't something more nefarious going on besides the CFE gas lines having a domino effect. He took a couple engineering booklets to the front of the sub-division and two of the other teenagers left to try and find a way to build a security fence.

The afternoon of day two came around and the three of them, less Sunny, were eating dinner. Everyone remained quiet until Amelia couldn't stay silent any longer.

"Sunny is really powerful." She blurted out.

The two guys looked over at her, questioning what she was saying.

"I know I am crazy, but she is like super powerful. She brought the rainstorm down on everyone and saved the houses. She's a hero."

Sam shook his head back and forth but didn't say anything. Anthony wasn't as smart.

"I can't believe you believe that stuff Amelia, it's such phooey." Anthony took a couple more bites of the food before he pushed his plate away.

"It is not Anthony and I am going to help her. I am going to prove to you both and then who will be eating their words." She pushed her chair back from the table and stormed off, marching right upstairs. It was time for her alone time with Sunny anyway, who needed men, certainly not them!

Amelia spent at least a few hours of each day sitting on Sunny's bed stroking the child's hair, reading her a book or other general motherly concerns for the young girl. She had watched the girl's body go from a typical coloring to pale white in a matter of twenty minutes. The darker the clouds became outside the less color Sunny had. If Amelia was honest with herself, or anyone, she would say that Sunny scared her. Not in the way that she was afraid for her safety, but in the way that she was scared for their future as a family with the obvious power surging in the girl's veins.

"Amelia" Sunny's throat sounded horse as she spoke.

"Yeah sweetie."

"Please don't make me leave."

That was all she said before she went back to sleep. Amelia knew as soon as Sunny was awake she and Sam would have to sit down with her and discuss what their relationship was developing into. Even if the two of them didn't work out as boyfriend and girlfriend she wouldn't kick them out. They were all in this together.

By the end of the third day Amelia had prepared dinner for the three teenagers. She had asked Anthony for an update on what was going on in the neighborhood.

"The Wilkinson house three doors down was a jackpot. Sadly no one survived probably because all their kids were older. I found them all sitting in the living room dead. But their garage and kitchen had a ton of stuff. We have distributed all the excess supplies we found evenly among all of the families."

"Like socialist do." Amelia jokingly said.

"Yes, actually." Sam responded.

"What?" Amelia now seemed confused.

"We men have been discussing it and we all agree the only way our community will maintain its safety is if we treat it like socialism."

"So now you're Josef Stalin?" Amelia said curtly.

Anthony palmed his face and shook his head back and forth. "I told you not to tell it to her like that, she never gets being subtle."

"We are all going to share responsibilities as a household. So, our house will be responsible for a certain portion and the next house the next thing. Individual houses will be responsible for their whole items as a family. But the community will depend on each other."

Amelia nodded, "Okay can you give me an example."

Anthony then continued for Sam, "Yeah. So, our house is responsible for infrastructure development and implementation."

"Gee just give us the hardest crap ever." Amelia rolled her eyes.

"In a way yes." Sam said.

Anthony chimed in "But in other ways no, we have the hard part at first, but after it's done, it's just maintaining."

"Okay I am listening." She stated, looking at them with a bit more patience.

The two guys continued to explain their plan. How they would develop a way to collect rain water by creating a water tower. The neighborhood agreed to move all the living families to the houses next to one another. There were six collective families counting them. So, three houses on each side would be occupied. The other houses were going to be used for practical things. Like look out's, storage, supplies.

Since no one lived in the two houses at the end of the street they would disassemble those homes for supplies to build the water tower.

"One of the other teens parents worked for a construction company who had a job-site not too far away. They have access to forklifts, dozers and other equipment on their job-site. He even had his parent's keys and access to the supplies. Tomorrow we are all going to the site and bringing back the heavy machinery to start their build out." Sam explained to her.

"Wait a moment." Amelia interjected. "You're telling me that you two are leading a construction crew now?"

Both guys grinned ear to ear. "Yep," they said in unison.

Amelia sighed, "And what is my role in all of this?"

The guys shook their heads no, Sam spoke. "None. We want you taking care of our home and Sunny. Whatever you think we need here is your purview. You have a hundred percent control of our house."

She had to admit that wasn't what she was expecting but she did like the sound of it.

"We're going to need to set up water to our house first." She stated.

They both nodded. "We're one step ahead of you." Sam said. "First we will make our own water tank in the back yard separate as a backup at night while the others aren't watching."

"Why in secret?" She asked.

Anthony spoke, "Because at the end of the day we want to make sure our family is safe above all else."

The two guys looked at each other in a certain way that made Amelia nervous.

"What aren't you two telling me?" Amelia looked between the two of them, "You can't keep me in the dark."

Sam looked to Anthony and then said, "It's about the other night."

"You mean the fire being controlled?"

"We worry about Sunny." Sam finally said. "If anyone found out about her, they would probably try and hurt her or us. So, we want to make sure our home is re-fortified just in case we end up back on our own and with enemies all around us."

Nodding Anthony continued, "Even if we don't understand the ability or how she can even do it, or any of the situation we know Sunny, we know her heart and we know she is good. We have to make sure we always protect her."

"Oh." Amelia said softly. "I hadn't thought about that." Her voice almost sounded meek as she spoke.

The three of them ate their food in silence for a few minutes thinking about what was just talked about. Their silence was broken when Sunny's weak voice said.

"Maybe you all should leave me somewhere else."

All three of their heads turned in her direction and said no emphatically at the same time.

"I don't want to hurt anyone." She mumbled to them.

"And you won't sweetie. Come on come eat." Amelia quickly said, as she stood up and walked over to her placing their hands together. "I promise Sunny."

Amelia put together a plate of food for Sunny, she added an extra serving thinking she would be famished from the energy exerted putting out the fire.

The four of them spend the rest of the meal in silence. All of them knew the weight of the situation, even though they hadn't talked about the elephant in the room.

"You know the big benefit, right?" Sam said to Amelia as they lay in the back yard looking up at the stars together later that night.

Their hands were intertwined together, and shoulders were touching as their backs pressed against the wool blanket that was their only barrier against the cool ground.

"I am scared to ask what benefit you found."

"We will never be without water."

"Excuse me?" Amelia laughed. "How do you figure?"

"Sunny." Sam laughed, as he said his cousin's name.

Sam didn't need to say anything else. Amelia knew what he was talking about.

"It's scary isn't it?" She eventually said.

"Yeah, but it is also cool."

"Has she always been able to do that?"

Sam shook his head back and forth, "No clue. No one I have ever known can do that. How about you, know anyone?"

Amelia giggled again, "No way, I thought that stuff was only in movies."

"She is scared you can see it on her." Sam's observation was mirrored by all of them. They were all scared of not just Sunny having power but the implication of what the power could lead to.

"There isn't anything we can do about it other than keep her safe." Amelia pulled his hand to her heart and held onto it more tightly. "Can we change the subject?" She asked.

"Of course." He turned onto his side propping himself up with his arm. "What's up?"

"Anthony talked to me this morning before you were awake."

Sam rolled his eyes, "He talked to me the other day too."

"I don't want anyone to get hurt Sam. I love Anthony, he's my twin. And I love Sunny too, like a little sister."

"Amelia, I am not planning on hurting you. Don't you know that?"

She agreed, "Yes but we're only almost eighteen, hardly the age to make such huge declarations."

"Not that huge, it isn't like I said I love you."

Her eyes widened at the words he just said. She held her breath for a few moments and then managed to whisper out, "Do you?"

She watched patiently as Sam sat there blinking a couple times and then looking down. She saw his arm start to move then he took her hand into his and brought it up to his lips to kiss.

"Amelia, I have loved you for about four years now. How's that for a declaration."

It was her turn to sit there and blink. What was she supposed to say to that?

"We've been friend's all our lives. How do you know it's been four years?"

An evil grin passed over Sam's lips, "Because that's when you got boobs."

Amelia screeched a laugh and then playfully slapped Sam's chest calling him a leech. After they rolled around playfully laughing and tickling each other Sam held her under him. His weight mostly balanced on the ground and not on her. "When did you know you loved me?" He asked in a soft-spoken tone.

"I never said that I did." She quipped back teasingly.

"It's your eyes; they say it every time I am in the room with you."

"About a year now." She said quietly.

"Oh, why a year?"

It was her turn to grin, "Because that's when Jenny Longer and I noticed that your arms started to have muscle."

"You're just as bad as I am!" Sam noted, and then he leaned his head down and kissed her. Their lips locked and for a few moments nothing happened. Then Amelia pushed her body off the ground and rolled Sam over onto his back with her on top of him. She placed her hands on either side of his face and held him in place. They laid there making out under the stars for who knew how long. It was their first time saying they loved one another. They wanted to tune out the entire world's problems and focus only on one another. At that moment, nothing else mattered. Not the explosion, the rain, the families in their care. Just the two of them.

Amelia's heart was racing, and she knew Sam's was too. She could feel it under his skin. His hand traveled down her back and found its way under her shirt. He only placed it on the small of her back, but it was flesh on flesh. His hand on her skin, in a place no one else had touched her. This made her body quiver with excitement. A feeling she had never felt before. The more they laid there together, the more she realized that being an adult and having a relationship was going to be more complicated than she originally thought. Because now she could also feel how much he was enjoying this too.

And that lead to a whole other slew of possibilities with Sam, that Amelia just wasn't ready to explore just yet.

Chapter Seven - One Year Later, Let There Be Light

NEARLY NINE MONTHS had passed since the group decided they would give the entire neighborhood electricity through solar panels. Sam spent almost two weeks at the library researching how to build a solar generator large enough to make this work. The group went through seven attempts before landing on one that could manage the entire neighborhood.

One of the other teens, now almost an adult, in the community, named John, his father owned the construction company. They went to his father's job sites and pilfered all the generators they could. It took the group a significant amount of time to understand the difference in the kilowatt hours that each generator produced. But the big problem with the ones they took, each machine required gasoline or diesel.

Eventually, they managed to find solar powered generators. After moving all the generators that they could Anthony and Sam found a way to transfer electricity to each house in the neighborhood. Anthony and Sam originally agreed, if they could simply pick up an item and implant it into their community, it would be easiest on all of them. As opposed to creating something from nothing. Anthony said he didn't see any reason to reinvent the wheel when they could just use a wheel from another source.

As it stood now, of the twenty homes that they saved, three became deconstructed and used to build the three cisterns. The main one located at the center of the subdivision which held the largest amounts of water. The second one was placed at the very back of the neighborhood of homes. An irrigation system was created and attached to it. John had found a solar timer at his father's job site that Sam converted to apply for this application. They made an automatic watering system that provided water to every home's garden. That way there was no need for anyone to remember to water their crop. If for whatever reason they didn't want to water their yard, they all had a shut off switch in their yards.

The third cistern was placed at the front of the community. The older teens all agreed that the younger children would need a safe place to play and congregate. Someone suggested making a playground. Amelia took that idea and expanded on it creating a play area that also maintained water fountains, water slides and other water activities. She argued that doing this would help with the summer heat, while making sure water for cooling off the children, became easily available.

John's sister Sarah had been in the same classes as Amelia in school. She questioned the sanitary conditions of the water. The two girls decided to create a water filtration system with homemade filters. So far most of the children enjoyed the playground. They built on the foundations of the previous homes. With John and the other guys using the construction equipment they were able to tear up the concrete slabs while reusing the pipes in the homes for the irrigation systems.

It almost seemed like a dream to all of them. That life somehow would snap back to their old reality one day. Sam would make comments about how he expected it to be like the zombie apocalypse era that grew in popularity, but it did not live up to the hype. They never found looters or stragglers. They just stayed to themselves.

Initially Anthony and Sam wanted Amelia to stay to their home and not worry about the community, but that didn't last. Her organization and obsessive-compulsive nature with crop rotation took over. She quickly claimed manager of the gardens. Everyone agreed that each plot of land would garden a specific crop. They would then rotate tilling the land. The homes that maintained people however would only hold gardens for those families. That way if they wanted something just for themselves they could. But everything harvested on the community home land would be split evenly between houses. She even developed a crop rotation schedule. They were now working through planting their third crop of fruits and vegetables.

With that same logic, Sam added water meters to each of the pipes leading into the homes where people lived. They implemented a daily limit of how much water would be consumed that way they would hopefully avoid a drought. The water flow would automatically shut off once the limit was reached and wouldn't re-open until the next day.

Sam and Anthony were glad they created their own water storage system in their back yard because of this. That way if they needed extra it was available.

Everyone, now a year older, had a life pattern that worked. They established a clear hierarchy and managed to get along with their small socialistic community. Sam and Sunny came up with a plan that if the weather didn't naturally deliver enough rain to them each week that she would supplement them at night while everyone slept. She felt nervous that someone would catch on, and none of them wanted that. Sometimes she would only make it rain in their own back yard.

The amount of control she gained with her power begun to make her want more.

Amelia had taken Sunny to the library every few weeks, so they could research psychic abilities and even witchcraft. No one knew exactly what Sunny had, but they all knew that it was special, and they wanted to protect that.

In the mist of the community development and camaraderie, John and Sam had developed a friendship. It was through this friendship that the community ended up having to develop a way to store meats, because both John and Sam both liked to hunt and fish together. They came up with a routine, that every third day the two of them would leave for twenty-four hours, to bring back as much animal meat or fish that they could. Anthony took the responsibility of ensuring enough freezers to keep the meat through winter. Even though they were in Florida that didn't mean animals would roam by daily during the cooler months.

It wasn't until the second Thanksgiving after the event, the reference the group had started referring to it as, happened that Anthony finally felt comfortable with Sam and Amelia being a couple. The community had decided to celebrate together, the guys created a make shift dining hall in the middle of the street. They had acquired tents, tables, chairs and decorated the whole area. The ladies took command of the food and prepared a feast fit for a king.

Anthony had stood back in the shadow and intently watched Amelia and Sam interact. He noticed how she would smile as he spoke and how Sam would hold her tenderly. He was happy for his sister and best friend, but at the same time he also felt stabs of jealousy.

"Penny for your thoughts?"

Anthony's head abruptly turned toward the direction of the voice and when it landed on Sarah he stiffened up.

"No, just minding my own business." He said.

"Not what it looks like," Sarah teased at him.

"Oh, what would you know what it looks like anyway?" He said in a harsher tone than he intended.

"You don't think I know that look? How long have we all gone to school together?"

"Long enough" Anthony grumbled.

Sarah nodded, "Yeah, long enough. I just can't figure out if that face you're making is aimed at her or him. I assume you're not mad at your BFF for having a girl now to hang with. But I suppose you could be mad that said girl is your twin. Or maybe that's it, you're mad your twin is now hanging with your BFF. Maybe you're scared of being replaced?"

"Leave me alone." He snapped.

"Yep that's it, I hit a nerve."

Sarah took a hand full of olives off the table she stood next to and started eating them. One by one she put them in her mouth. She made enough of a distraction that eventually Anthony could only focus on her mouth and what she was doing with it. He had a vague feeling that she was speaking to him, but he wasn't listening.

"Hello!" She said a little louder. "Earth to Anthony." She was now waiving her hand in front of his face and snapping her fingers.

"Sorry." He said, shaking his head back and forth, "I was distracted."

Sarah laughed, and smiled at him. "Distracted, yeah I would say so."

Anthony gave her a sideways smile as he moved his head around his neck in a moment of discomfort.

"You know you could get back at them instead of just staying angry right."

"What are you talking about Sarah?"

She smiled at him and walked closer, closing the space between them. "You could get back at them. Show them that they aren't the only ones who can find love after the event happened."

"And how do you suppose I do that?" He inquired.

"Like this." Sarah walked up to him and wrapped her arms around his neck, she leaned in towards his head. Anthony quickly placed his hands on her hips and met her half way, leaning in for the kiss.

He had forgotten all together that they were standing in the tent where the whole community would be able to see, until he heard someone making kissing sounds at them. Sarah pulled away from Anthony and he looked past her shoulder to see Sunny as the culprit. The brat.

"Happy Thanksgiving Anthony. I hope we can do that again." Sarah popped another olive in her mouth, and smiled at him before returning to the table where she had her plate of food waiting on her. Next to her brother John. Who was now staring at Anthony in the same tone that he had been previously staring at Sam not five minutes before.

Anthony felt his neck start to redden, he attempted to brush off the teasing from the seven-year-old and walked back to his seat. Sam and Amelia didn't comment but his sister did smile at him. Maybe Sarah was right, he could do this.

Two weeks later the group's resilience was put to the test. They had taken for granted previously the idea that the news and government sent out warnings before hurricanes hit. But they learned quickly that only applied when you had Doppler technology and a meteorologist who could predict what was going to happen. The winds that sprung up were so strong that the cistern at the front of the complex was the first to come down. The guys hadn't finished reinforcing the frame and now they were going to have to rebuild it completely.

Throughout their neighborhood debris was moving across the streets. There had never been a high priority for trash removal since the group typically burned all the waste they produced. Consequently, they never cleaned up the remains of the homes that burned and the trash from all the construction.

"Everyone needs to take shelter!" Anthony yelled out on the bull horn, as he ran down the streets alerting everyone to the danger.

Everywhere he stepped there was some hazard. What scared him the most was the rebar that was lose around the neighborhood. He didn't know how strong the wind would need to travel to pick the rebar up. But if that happened it would be a deadly weapon. Water started to pour down in sheets. The rain had started mid-morning on a Tuesday. There was no build up with sprinkles or light showers. Mother Nature dropped a full-on down pour just eighteen hours after the winds had hit shore.

The onslaught lasted for two days straight with no let up. Sunny stayed in her room crying which they were convinced was making the hurricane more intense. Truthfully, they didn't know if it was a hurricane or a tropical storm but with the amount of rain that flooded the roads and the wind speed they believed it was a hurricane.

"Sunny, sweetie you have to stop crying." Amelia tried coaxing and soothing techniques to calm the young girl, but nothing seemed to work.

"She will stop when she is ready. Maybe the storm is making her do it. We don't know how her ability works." Anthony said.

"I am not used to you being so level headed." Amelia playfully teased her brother.

"Two weeks with Sarah and he's cool as a cucumber. It's a miracle." Sam grinned at Anthony as he stated his little barb.

"Knock it off you two it isn't that at all. It's the fact that I have faith in our little Sunny."

She heard him and turned her head in the direction of his voice. Anthony smiled at her reassuringly. "Yeah Sunny, that's right. I have faith in you. I know that when it's time you will stop this storm. You're not making it worse."

Sam and Amelia exchanged glances with one another then looked at Sunny. Her facial coloring had begun to lighten. It was bright red at the peak of her tears and she had been almost feverish. Amelia reached her hand out to feel for the temperature and even that had already begun to lessen.

"You're right Anthony, I am not trying to." She wiped her eyes and walked over to him.

"I know you're not. But it's okay, you cry as much as you need to." Anthony and Sunny stayed in her room watching the weather. Her tears had slowed from nonstop to light streams running down her face.

Sam pulled on Amelia's hand to move them out of the room and whispered to her on the way out, "When did aliens abduct your brother?"

"Hey, I heard that!" Anthony hollered out.

"Good!" Sam shot back.

Shortly after the light family banter the rain had stopped, and the clouds began to clear up. No one wanted to go outside and assess the damage. They were all scared to see what would require to be rebuilt. Anthony feared it all would be gone.

After some of the water drained off, and the sun was completely out, it was safe to venture outside. A silent hush fell over the neighborhood and individually each of the families walked out of their homes and began assessing damage. All in all, they lost one garden completely, half of two, the one cistern and some miscellaneous other structural items. It could have been a lot worse. It was going to take at least a week for the land to dry out before they could start rebuilding structural items on them.

The younger kids still looked frightened only a few hours after the storm. Their playground had been washed away and were feeling distraught over that. They all understood how the younger kids were feeling and no one commented. As a group, they decided after walking around and assessing damage, the best thing to do would be go back to their homes and wait until morning. The men would fix everything, and the women would take care of the young children inside.

A tide had shifted with the group. Amelia couldn't place her finger on it but something important had changed. She just didn't know if that something was for the better, or not.

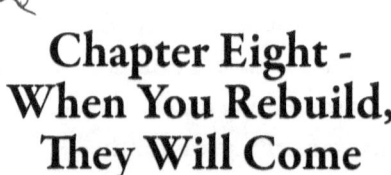

Chapter Eight -
When You Rebuild,
They Will Come

WITH ANTHONY AND JOHN leading the pack the two of them set out towards more construction sites looking for gear. When they encountered their first issue was when they realized it was harder the second time around.

"I don't understand, why is this forklift not starting? It has diesel in it and everything." Anthony stated in an exasperated tone.

"How would I know, I never worked the sites." John responded with as he opened the hood of the forklift and started looking around.

"Do you even know what you're doing?"

John shrugged his shoulders, "How hard could it be, fiddle with this and fiddle with that. It is bound to turn on."

"You don't want to make it worse, hey maybe it got flooded?" Anthony now was walking around the machine and looking at the tires, trying to determine if he could indicate a flood line.

"It wasn't flooded look how high off the ground this engine is. Water wasn't that high at our house."

The two of them continued to tinker when they heard someone approaching. Their heart rates picked up and anxiously they turned around to see a young woman looking back at them. Her hair was as red as fire and her hips were plump and round. She had the body of a goddess and she was coming right towards them.

"It needs primed." She stated flatly, while glaring at them.

"What's that?" Anthony asked.

"Primed, you know something they do to machines when they stop working."

"And do you know how to do that?" John said.

"Maybe. What's in it for me?" She was walking closer to them now and began to smile.

Both guys started to act nervous and as she approached they looked back and forth at each other. "What is it you want?" Anthony finally said. He didn't want to come across as a jerk, but he didn't want to give away too much before they knew more about her.

"My friends and I are looking for a place to stay. We've been living here. Where do you stay?"

John immediately started to respond when Anthony put his hand on his arm to silence him. "How many are there with you and your friends, and how old?"

"Well I am nineteen and then there is my sister who is eleven then my brother and I don't know maybe five or so others. Varying ages. You have room?"

"Give us a moment." John stated and then leaned in close to Anthony. "What should we do? We can't leave them out here in an old run-down construction job site."

"But we don't know them John, we can't just invite strangers into our home."

"That's what you did with me and the rest of the neighborhood." John said calmly.

"Not really, we all lived in the same place for years and we went to school together." Anthony looked the stranger up and down again and then turned back to John. "Why don't we see what all she can offer? You know how we live in our community. We all provide something."

John nodded in agreement and then spoke up, "What's your name?"

The woman smiled at them, "Natalie."

"Natalie, I'm John and this is my friend Anthony. We want to know, what could you and your friends offer our community?"

"What do you mean offer?"

Anthony spoke up, "You see, we have what you could call a socialistic neighborhood. We all pitch in and help. Then we share equally in the profits of whatever emerges from the effort."

"So, you are all Russian?" Natalie laughed.

The two guys shrugged their shoulders up and down, "I guess so, in the way we are operating."

"How long have you two been doing this?" She asked.

"Since shortly after the event happened basically." John stated as a matter of fact. "It works, Anthony is our leader there."

That made Anthony pause a second and look at his friend before responding, "Before we potentially endanger our families we want to make sure it's a good fit and that there aren't any freeloaders."

"I see," Natalia tapped her hand on her hip and stood there for a moment assessing them. "What kind of skills do you currently have?"

John spoke up first, "We have hunters, me and our buddy Sam, and we have crops ran by his sister. Water filtration my sister heads up. And..."

Anthony cut him off before he could disclose any more of their home. "I'll tell you what, why don't you tell me your skills and I will tell you if there is room for you. Okay?"

Natalie let out a laugh and nodded, "I get ya. Basically, my dad, his dad and my brother all were mechanics. So, I grew up in a shop. I know a lot of the basic maintenance stuff like oil changes and tire rotations. I was in the process of learning about injector systems and flushing them when my family died. But I saved my dad's mechanic books and have been studying. I also can work on construction equipment." She pointed out the forklift that the two guys were still standing by. "Same concept different machines." She looked between the two of them. "Do you have any need for a mechanic? If you don't have vehicles the technical skills work on other things like mowers or AC units. Assuming you have electricity."

Anthony was interested, and he whispered to John, "Would a mechanic be worth giving up an entire house for and adding eight more mouths to care for?"

He replied in the same whispered tone, "I don't know. We really could use one, but that is a lot of responsibility to add."

While the two guys discussed more details alone, Natalie called out, "You know I'm not the only one with skills, we have a doctor."

Anthony's head shot up, "How do you have a doctor?"

"Well, not a doctor per say ... her folks were both doctors and she was a volunteer at the hospital. She is nineteen too and had just gotten her a license, whatever that stands for."

"You sure seem to have all your bases covered there don't you Natalie." John smirked at her as he spoke.

"Sure do, so what do you say?" Natalie walked closer and extended her hand in Anthony's direction. "Partnership?"

"Before we agree to anything you will need to first agree to the rules of our community. It's important that the status quo is maintained because we have twenty people relying on our choices."

"Well hit me with it Anthony, tell me what it's like."

The two of them took an hour to explain to Natalie all the different facets of their community. She appeared impressed with all they told her of how they divided up the tasks and created an infrastructure that almost withstood the hurricane entirely.

"I have lots of solar powered stuff." Natalie said, at the end of their explanation.

"How is that possible?" Anthony asked.

"Here let me show you." Natalie gestured for the two of them to follow her and that's what they did.

She led them towards the back where the construction job trailers were located. There she opened the lock and asked them to come inside. When they crossed the threshold they were amazed by how much she truly did own. There were stock piles of water and Gatorade. She had rechargeable batteries and solar chargers. Flashlights, blankets, canned food and more.

"How did you get all this stuff?" Anthony asked.

"I've been traveling job site to job site looking for these items. I figured what we didn't use I would be able to trade off."

"Where are the others with you, obviously they aren't living here."

She shook her head, "No, they are living in a house across the street. We didn't want to stay on site incase trouble happened."

"Smart. Okay well I think it is safe if your doctor friend agrees. Two skilled workers in exchange for 6 others to tag along. You all will have to share a house though. And you will be given a garden to maintain for the community. In addition to mechanical and doctor like tasks. Your own yard may contain whatever you like. We suggest to everyone that they maintain their own private garden as well."

Natalie confirmed, "That seems like fair terms. Maybe I can help your sister with the filtration system too, or reinforcing the towers. I am really good at that type of work as well."

John's eyebrows raised up in excitement when Natalie said that. Anthony could see the future clear as day as if it was written on the wall. Pretty soon everyone would need a boyfriend or a girlfriend. He supposed that seemed about right. It was the apocalypse, why not have a special friend to go through it with.

"You know this is all well and good, but we still need that forklift to start up, so we can fix the cistern." Anthony said, as he brought the room back to reality.

"Oh, that's easy, I disassembled the starter plug."

"I thought you said it needed a prime or whatever."

"Yeah I lied, I didn't know you two then. We use that forklift to move around and get things we want. It is in top order. As are most of the machines at that site."

"John, are you thinking what I am thinking?"

He nodded, "I think so Anthony."

"And what's that, boys?"

Anthony replied matter of factually, "If we took all of these pieces of equipment back to our home we could reinforce our walls better and make our subdivision more secure."

"That's not what I was thinking!" John laughed, "I was thinking if we took these back with us clean up would be a hell of a lot easier on everyone!"

Anthony chuckled and grinned at John, "Well that is clearly true, but I was thinking long term."

"Sure, we can take them. We can go get the others and caravan to your neighborhood."

"Sounds like a plan." Anthony pushed his arm out towards her and grinned, "Now you have yourself a deal."

Amelia and Sarah had spent all morning rebuilding their water filtration system for the children's play area. They had to improvise since some of the parts had been broken beyond repair. After more than three hours sitting on the ground and working on the rebuild they both were exhausted.

"So, my brother huh?" Amelia had said as she finished fixing her last part.

"Seems that way." Sarah shrugged her shoulders, "I don't know what we're doing exactly, but it's fun."

"He seems to think you two are an item and well onto your way of spending the rest of the apocalypse together."

This comment made Sarah laugh, "It's safe to say that right now we are getting to know each other on a deeper level and we are enjoying each other's company, yes."

"There are not many available guys." Amelia stated.

"Is that what's going on with you and Sam, availability?"

"That's totally different." She said back in a curt manner.

"How so?" Sarah had a gleam in her eye, she was enjoying torturing Amelia.

"For starters we had been dancing around this for a while now. He's my brother's best friend it wasn't something I was going to just wake up and do, ya know."

"Sure, I know, but you did, wake up and do it. So now what?"

It was Amelia's turn to shrug.

Sarah looked her friend in the eye, "Do you love him?" She asked softly.

Amelia made the yes motion with her head, "I really do."

"Then you'll marry him."

"What?" Amelia asked disbelievingly. "We are way too young to get married."

"How so? Best any of us can tell no one over eighteen survived the event. That makes us all adults. That's what adults do, they get married and have kids." She started humming the song, *Here Comes the Bride* teasing Amelia.

"I am not ready to jump into that. And Sam has never mentioned anything of that to me."

"You all live in the same house, you've kidding me, right?"

"I am not, we don't even have sex." Amelia stopped in her statement and looked at Sarah with a hard and stern expression. "Do you and my brother?"

"What Anthony and I do is our business, but no." She said grinning at her friend.

Amelia burst into laughter and clapped her hands together, "Oh boy you had me scared there for a second I thought you were going to tell me you two were discussing long term future goals."

"Oh, we do discuss the future."

"Really?"

Sarah nodded up and down, "Yes, just usually it involves whatever crazy scheme he wants to add to the community. Lately he has been trying to figure out a way to make the telephones work again. Don't ask me why he thinks we need them."

"Oh," Amelia wasn't sure what she should say. The whole discussion had taking an odd turn she wasn't really prepared to stomach so she let the subject matter drop.

After Sarah and Amelia were done cleaning up their work area they began walking back to their own homes. As Amelia opened her front door she was stopped at the sight of Sunny and Sam playing a card game. She recognized it was a game of Go Fish and that warmed her heart. He was extremely attentive to his little cousin and she found that very endearing.

"Hey guys, room for a third?" She asked them smiling.

"Yes! Sunny here is killing me, I could use the help." Sam winked at her and patted the ground next to where he was sitting.

"Sam is letting me win, but yes please join in." Sunny moved her lips up in the form of a smile at her and Sam as she spoke.

"I'm not letting you win, you're just really good."

Amelia laughed at the two of them and waited patiently to be dealt into the next game. She was looking at the situation differently now. Looking at Sam differently. What would happen in the next five years? Were they going to be expected to get married? Would Sam even want that? She knew her mom would have a fit if she even heard this mental conversation going on right now, but possibly Sarah was right. They needed to think about these things.

"What are you thinking about?" Sam asked her.

"Sarah and I were just talking about the future, so I was just trying to picture things in five years."

"Oh, that sounds like a deep convo, glad I wasn't involved."

His response pretty much answered her own questions she hadn't had a chance to even mentally voice to herself. He wasn't thinking of the future at all. What did that mean for them and the community?

"So, you don't think about the future at all?" Amelia questioned.

"In some regard of course," he paused to look at Sunny and smiled, "got to make sure we have rain water to survive, right kiddo."

"That's right," Sunny winked at her cousin as she said it.

Amelia loved how much Sam took care of Sunny. He didn't make it seem like a burden or something he was angry about. That was one of the things she did love about him, how he took care of family. But she couldn't help thinking that they were far too young to even begin thinking about a future together as a couple. Getting through these uncertain times needed to be the priority and she was determined to see that it was done correctly.

"Hey Sam," Amelia said.

"Yeah sweetie?" His reply was soft and caring.

"How about we go out tonight, just you and me."

"Sure, where do you want to go?"

"I want to find a church." She wasn't even sure why that came out of her mouth, but it did. And it felt right.

"Weird, but okay. Once John and Anthony get back we can go out together."

"What about me?" Sunny whined.

"What about you, ya little monster." Sam teased his cousin.

"No one takes me out, I'm always left alone."

"Tomorrow night I'll take you out, just you and me kid, I promise." Sam reached his hand out towards Sunny in an attempt to get her to shake hands.

She looked at his hand like she was analyzing it, "Deal." She shook his hand in return and then pulled the next card from the deck and smiled. "Another pair, I think I've won Sam."

They all looked at the ground where Sunny had over twenty pairs displayed, and poor Sam only had three. "Yeah Sunny, I think you did." Amelia held back a laugh as she spoke. "Poor, poor Sam."

When the go-Fish game came to a close Sunny packed her cards up and ran upstairs to her room. Everyone in the house had grown accustom to Sunny spending most of her free time up there. It was something about the peace and quiet of her own space that recharged her inner spark. No one talked about it, it was just something they all acknowledged.

"What about the future had you thinking so hard?" Sam asked, as he tapped his finger on his leg nervously.

Sarah had sparked ideas in Amelia's head and she didn't want to over analyze or put too much pressure on Sam.

"Just stuff, you know, the usual." She said simply.

"Nothing about the current here and now is usual. That could literally mean anything. Do you not want to talk?"

Did she want to talk? She could be upfront and honest with him and risk losing what they have. Or the exact opposite could happen. "Not that I don't want to..." she said.

"That was a lot of negatives. I am sure Mrs. Reed back in English II would have a cow at that sentence. Isn't that a double negative or something?"

Amelia shook her head, "No it wasn't. That would be like, 'not never I don't want' or something like that."

"Guess this is why Anthony made the A's in English and not us, ain't it?"

"Isn't it," Amelia corrected.

"You're dodging my question, just spit it out." Sam was sitting cross legged looking directly at her now. It was obvious his full attention was devoted on whatever Amelia was going to say.

She felt regret building up before she even spoke, with a heavy sigh she spit it out, "She asked me if we were going to get married and have kids."

"You told her yes, right?" Sam's facial features hadn't changed a bit. He was still staring at her with his intense facial features glued to her.

Amelia couldn't believe what she had heard. Her mouth gaped open before responding. "No, I told her we weren't thinking about the future."

"Yes, we are." Sam moved his arm out and let his hand rest on hers. "I think about it all the time with you."

"But we don't talk about it, ever."

Sam smiled at her, "Isn't it kind of a given. I mean, we've been dancing around us forever."

"Now that I did tell her, glad we agree on one thing." Amelia was smiling at her boyfriend. A true genuine smile. "But we are kids, we aren't in any place to think about that kind of future."

"Why aren't we? We're the oldest ones left alive. Back in the old days we would be married and having babies at our age. We're almost twenty now."

"No, we aren't, we are barely nineteen." Amelia amended.

"Whichever, you would have been married at thirteen in some cultures. So, it is normal for us to think about it. Hell, I have known I wanted to marry you for years. You took my breath away a long time ago."

"How would that even work, we live with my brother and your cousin?"

"You don't think Anthony is going to want to marry Sarah?" Sam picked up her hand and brought his head down closer, so he could place a kiss on the back of it.

"I don't know," Amelia sighed. "Like I told her, I've never really given it any thought. Besides, they are still new, we at least have a little mileage under us."

The two of them sat in silence on the floor for a few minutes. Their hands entwined together as the moments ticked by. Amelia was too scared to speak. She hadn't meant to dive into this train of thought just yet. What he and Sarah were saying made sense, about their age and marriage. But she still felt like a child.

As luck would have it, she didn't have to say anything else because Anthony walked in the door. "Guys, do I have a surprise for you!"

Chapter Nine -
Times Are Changing

ANTHONY WALKED INTO the house followed closely by John and then Natalie. He wasn't sure what he had just walked in on with his sister and friend, but it had looked serious. Good he didn't want them getting too serious.

"Amelia, I have someone you're going to want to meet." He waited for his sister to stand up and then he introduced them. "This is Natalie and she is a mechanic. Her friend Jody is a doctor."

Amelia extended her hand and shook Natalie's when she grabbed it. With a confused look she said, "It's nice to meet you. But how do you have a doctor friend?"

"Hi Amelia, your brother talked about you the whole way here. And as I explained to him already she was the daughter of two doctors and had received her CNA license before all hell broke loose. So, she is like a doctor."

"Ahh. That makes more sense. Either way we are glad to have your skills here in our group. I am sure we can find a small house you two could use."

John smiled, and Anthony shook his head. "They are going to need the McGwire's old place."

Amelia gave her brother another puzzled look, "Why, that is like a six-bedroom mini mansion two people don't need all that space."

"We actually have eight total." Natalie politely stated.

"Eight!" Amelia exclaimed.

Before she could say anything, else Sam shot up and interjected, "Hi, I'm Sam. I live here in this place with them. It's nice to meet you."

Natalie grinned, "I am glad to meet you too."

Anthony regained control of the conversation, "Yes they have eight people. John and I explained how our community works, and in exchange for her mechanical skills and the medical skills we are accepting their six others as part of our group. It seems like a fair trade since I know you and Sarah have issues manning all the mechanical stuff. I thought you would be happy."

Amelia regained her composure she always tried to use when dealing with people outside of her family. "Well, yeah that does seem very fair and you're right I hate dealing with all of that. Did you explain the water rations?"

"Water rations?" Natalie inquired.

It was Sam's turn to explain, "Yes we have water lines running to each of our houses and gardens. Each house is allotted so much water a day. If you hit the limit the meter automatically shuts off. It is very useful in keeping things even and no one taking advantage of anyone else's hard work."

"Wow that sounds fair. I hadn't realized when you said cistern earlier Anthony it was because you all had water piped into the houses. That is kind of amazing."

Anthony, Sam and Amelia all three beamed with pride. They had done amazing things in order to make their community work.

Anthony spoke next, "Like I told you earlier, you're responsible for whatever you want in your own garden. We have planted our favorite items and we have a miniature cistern we maintain that way we can do extra laundry or take longer bathes if we want. You're welcome to do that as well."

John stepped in, "We only ask that if you build something that isn't for the community just yourselves then you collect the resources for that item from material that you scavenge. That way you're not taking it away from the group as a whole."

"That seems fair," Natalie nodded her head again.

"Tomorrow we can introduce the rest of your group to everyone. For now, I am going to take you over to the McGwire's place and get you all settled in." Anthony looked at Sam, "It's all set up right piped for water and electric?"

"Yes sir, everything is piped and ready just have to turn the switch on."

"Sounds good," Anthony signaled with his hand for Natalie to follow him, he turned to his sister and friend, "Flip the switch will ya? I will see you in the morning, I am staying at Sarah's tonight." And with that command he walked out of the house with John and Natalie following behind him.

"**W**ell that was quite a turn of events wouldn't you say." Sam looked at Amelia.

"Yeah, it really was. Let's go flip the switch and then we can come back and relax." Amelia didn't appear like she wanted to relax. She looked like she was ready to scream, probably because of all the drama that had just transpired in the last ten minutes.

The two of them walked from their house over to the cistern, and Amelia waited on the ground as Sam climbed his way to the top. She had no way of following him because the standing area wasn't large enough. She gazed up at the top of the tower with her hand over her eyes trying to focus on the body she saw now moving along the small walkway.

"Everything okay?" She called out to him from the ground. She saw him turn slightly and look in her direction from about thirty feet in the air.

"Yeah it's going good just finding which valve it is. I have to decode my system."

Amelia took the time alone on the ground to think about what she wanted to say to him when they went back to the house to relax. She knew she loved him, she could feel it inside her bones. She knew that especially for what they were living through she had it really well and trusted Sam completely. This mental strain she felt was on her end and not his. She saw his eyes when he looked at her, it had love in them.

She was so entrapped in her thoughts that she didn't even notice Sam walking back towards her.

"Penny for your thoughts Amelia?"

The sound of his voice made her jump in her spot and she used her hand to reach for her heart to calm her nerves, "Sam, I didn't see..." She stopped talking when she saw the look in his eye. He almost looked mischievous.

"You didn't see what?" He asked as he took steps towards her, cutting the distance between them quickly.

"I didn't, well never mind." She tried to brush it off. "Let's go home."

"Wait," Sam reached his hand out and grabbed Amelia's before she could turn towards the house. "Let's stay, together tonight."

"Sam, we stay together every night."

"Let's stay together out here tonight." He pulled her closer to him, "Alone."

His voice soft in tone and sultry sounding. She knew he would try to kiss her, before he did she let him take her face in his palms and tilt her head up to meet his. Sam's lips were soft to kiss, she always enjoyed it. After a few stolen moments she broke the embrace and stepped back from him.

"We can't, my brother is at Sarah's we have to stay with Sunny." She watched the recognition of her words register and she swore she saw sadness creep into his appearance for a quick moment.

"Another night then." He moved in her direction and still holding hands they returned to their home.

Sunny watched from her window at her cousin down on the street. She didn't understand what bothered her about the scene, but she knew something was off. There was something about all of it that made her sad and the more she watched her cousin the harder it was to accept. She felt like she was an outsider even though she was family. Amelia was very nice to her and she loved her like a sister, but she was taking Sam away from her.

They both had told her over and over she would never be alone but Sunny knew one day she would be. The feeling inside her grew sad and dark. She knew jealousy wasn't logical, but she couldn't hold it in. She had to let it out before she exploded, and it was at that moment she heard the thunder. Hopefully Sam and Amelia wouldn't know she caused the sound and come check on her. She was pretty sure she wouldn't be able to handle seeing them both together tonight.

She needed to run away. She had to get away. Sunny hadn't asked for any this. She hadn't asked to be a survivor, she wished she was with her parents right now. She missed them and needed to be close to them.

That was when she had the thought, the thought that would change her forever. She focused her concentration on one image, the image of her mother and father's wedding picture. She remembered when things were simple and good for them. Her mother baking brownies in the oven, her father and her building the treehouse. She needed to be home, where she could relive the memories she had just from a couple years ago.

Sunny felt the tears starting to trickle down her face, she couldn't hold them back and she could hear the impact it was having on the world around her. The thunder rumbling and the rain pelting against the window. She was tired of hiding away in her room. She closed her eyes and thought back to the memory of her mother and her skin felt the goose bump shivers start to form. It started at the base of her neck and traveled down her spine. Each vertebra they touched chilled and when she opened her eyes she realized she was home.

Back in her old room, the room her parents made her. She was sitting on her bed and her heart leapt into her throat as she held her breath, could it have all been a dream? Hurrying off of the bed she ran through her room, not even noticing that when she ran past her mirror there was no reflection of her body looking back at her.

She soared through the upstairs even though there were no lights. She knew the house like the back of her hand. As she turned the corner and ran down the stairs and found herself standing in the middle of her living room. As she looked around the room she noticed that someone had come into her home and taken things. The television was still there but the couches were missing. There was a clock on the wall that was no longer there.

Sunny had known she was crying but she couldn't feel any tears on her cheek. Her hand came up and her fingers touched her cheek, but she felt nothing. That was when she looked down at her hands and realized, she was translucent. She could see straight through her arms. With a gasp of air and a cry she ran to the bathroom on the first floor. The door was already open, so she walked right into the doorway and looked in the mirror. There was nothing looking back at her.

She had only heard of something like this in the book, *A Christmas Carol* with the Ghost of Christmas Past. Sunny started to panic when it all sank in slowly that she had somehow sent her mind or spirit away from her body. She felt herself suddenly being pulled through some sort of plane and she landed back in her room but this time on the floor. She looked around the room she had occupied for the last year, she was back home, her new home, not the old home she craved. Sunny's hands roamed over her body patting it down to make sure it was real. The sadness she felt from the loss of connection from her parents hit her hard, the tears this time she could feel as they ran down her cheeks.

"Sunny are you okay?" She heard Amelia yelling from down the hall.

They were coming her way, maybe they had heard her fall or could hear her crying. "Yes," she called out meekly.

Without notice her door opened with Amelia entering the room first followed closely by Sam. They were instantly by her side kneeling down next to her.

"Sam, I'm okay really." She protested, as he pulled her up onto the bed.

"We heard you fall Sunny, you were crying." Sam looked over her head, she assumed he was inspecting for a bump.

"I just tripped, come on, I'm fine." Sunny was pushing Sam's hands away from her body.

"Are your sure sweetie?" Amelia was kneeling next to the bed looking up at Sunny.

"Yes, I'm fine, leave me alone!" Sunny yelled this at Amelia and then she hopped off the bed and ran out of the room.

She didn't want to see them, she didn't want them to see her like this. Sunny was fully aware that she was over reacting to seeing them kiss and she didn't understand it. She just knew she couldn't see them. She grabbed her bag that she kept at the end of the stairs and ran out of the front door and into the night. She couldn't be home, she had to find freedom.

Sunny ran as fast as she could to the playground where the children all played. The rain on her back didn't bother her, it cooled her anger. She found the peace in the darkness with the lightning and thunder in the distance. She tried to focus her thoughts on the sound of her heart beating, slowing her tears and anger with each beating drum she heard in her head.

"Sunny? Sunny!" Sam's voice was coming through, despite the sounds of thunder ringing out.

"Sunny, where are you?" He kept calling out her name. If she didn't respond she knew the entire neighborhood would be outside looking for her. She tried to find her resolve inside her, but it wasn't there. She felt weak and broken.

"There you are!" Sam came running down the street towards her and she didn't move. She let him wrap his arms around her in a hug and hold her close.

"Sam," she started to say, and then stopped when he knelt eye level with her.

"Sunny, I love you so much. I don't know what has you so upset, but I am sorry if it was something we did."

She leaned her head into his shirt and cried. She let her grief and anger out; as the rain intensified she cried more. She wasn't sure if the rain was fueling her grief, but she knew the harder she cried the more she felt the pelts of rain against her back.

"Honey, talk to me sweetie, tell me what's wrong." Sam was trying to coax it out of her. She knew he cared and loved her.

"I'm mad at you and Amelia." She said in a voice that sounded like she was ashamed of her feelings.

"Why, what did we do?" Sam looked genuinely confused and Sunny knew she was going to have to be honest with him.

"I saw you two kissing outside tonight."

"Okay?" Sam questioned. "And that upset you?"

She nodded into his shirt and all she felt was his large arms wrapped around her, holding her close.

"Does it make you mad Amelia and I are together?"

"Not usually, it did tonight, though."

She let Sam pick her up and start carrying her back to their home. Out of the corner of her eye she noticed Anthony standing on the porch of someone's house watching the scene. Great, someone else who would know her shame. She pushed that thought aside as she and her cousin made their way home.

"I'm sorry." She said into his ear as he placed her on their porch.

"Sunny, sweetie, you don't have to apologize. We're the adults now, you're the kid. You don't have to apologize for having feelings and emotions. We should make sure to take everything you feel into consideration before we do stuff."

"You didn't do anything wrong." She was sniffling now, like a real little child, she hated that.

"Then why did it upset you, you seeing us kiss?"

"It's stupid I don't want to tell you."

Sam didn't force her to say anything, he just took her hand and walked into the house with her. "Amelia, I found her!"

Sunny watched Amelia come out of the kitchen and run up to her, grabbing her into a hug. Sunny's body went stiff but Amelia didn't let go. She just looked down at her and said, "I don't know what I did but I am sorry. In the future, don't run away, pull me aside and talk to me woman to woman, okay?"

She wiped her eyes and nose off on her arm nodding her head, "Okay Amelia."

"Good. Now, you both are dripping wet, how about you go change and I make everyone some hot chocolate and we can all play a board game?"

Sam was the first to speak, "That sounds great Am, but, how about we get the hot chocolate and Sunny and I play a game and you go read in bed?"

Amelia gave him a questioning look, Sunny knew what that meant but she didn't indicate she was mad. She smiled at them instead, "Alright, whatever you guys want. I have a new book I found in my moms' stuff I wanted to read anyway. Go on now, go dry off."

Sunny wasn't stupid, she knew that was too easy and tomorrow she would have to talk to Amelia about it. For now, though, she went off to her bathroom to clean off and change. She would figure out what to say to her in the morning. Right now, she had to decide if she was going to tell her cousin about what else happened tonight, not just the rage of jealousy.

"**I** just don't know what came over her." Sam said to Amelia as they walked into the kitchen together. "She said she saw us kissing tonight and that upset her."

"Ahh, I think I know what it is." Amelia said with a smile.

"Please clue me in."

"She's jealous."

"Sunny is my kid cousin, she doesn't want to date me Amelia."

"Not that kind of jealous you dolt, like Anthony was. She thinks I am taking you from her I bet. She is probably jealous of the extra time we are spending together. She has no one to do that with."

"Oh, well what can we do about that? I mean technically we're adults now, we have responsibilities in the community now. We need our time together."

Amelia nodded her head, but she thought about the words she wanted to use to explain this. "Think about it Sam. You have me, you also have Anthony. I have Anthony and you. Who does Sunny have?"

"She has all of us, we're a family. And if you and I get married like I want us to, she will be your family by rights not just by declaration."

"It isn't the same for her, she's a decade younger than us. She can't relate to us on the things we are doing. I think maybe we have made a mistake keeping her inside this whole time away from everyone. She has no friends Sam."

"We don't want people to find out about her powers. We have to keep her inside."

"Do we really? What if keeping her inside is causing her more harm than our community finding out we will never have to suffer from a drought? Isn't that kinda a big deal? Don't you think if that leaked out, there could be a lot worse revelations out there we don't know about?"

"I don't know Amelia. I love her and it's about keeping her safe."

"It's also about letting her grow up. We're growing up as you keep pointing out to me. We have to let her also. She needs to have someone she feels safe with, like you and I have."

"She isn't dating Amelia!"

"Did I say date? No! I said she needs a friend. Look talk it over with Anthony if you don't believe me. But look at him now, how happy is he since he found Sarah?"

"I guess, fine, okay."

"Good, now, go get changed. She is going to wonder where you are. I'll be fine, we can continue our conversation later. Maybe we can see if some of the new people we now have are her age. Get to know them."

"I'll leave that to you, you're better at the whole socializing thing."

"Glad you notice my positive traits. Now go, I'll read a book, I wasn't lying, I did find a book I want to read."

Sam leaned over and kissed Amelia on the lips lightly, "I do love you, you know."

She nodded as he kissed her and afterwards she responded, "I know, I love you too. Now shoo."

Once she got Sam out of the kitchen she let the whole conversation impact her. She felt horrible that she hadn't seen it coming. She knew at some point Anthony would get jealous, but she hadn't thought about Sunny. Maybe because it wasn't a sibling, but she should have seen it that way. They were all the family that each of them had.

She decided right then, that she would make a point to do more things with Anthony, so Sam and Sunny could have time together. Or she could do things on her own. There was the community Christmas to plan out. The Thanksgiving dinner had gone so well. She would need to plan out the crop rotations too. Without realizing what was happening her mind started to race. She went over to her desk and pulled out her notebook.

She made a few columns on a page and began the menu for Christmas.

Amelia was deep into thought figuring out how much of the crop would need to be stored in order to feed the growing number of mouths at the dinner. She was engrossed in her work and didn't hear the front door open until Anthony had called her name.

"Hey Amelia. Everything okay?" Anthony was shaking his umbrella out and placing it against the wall.

"Hey and yeah, Sunny just had a hard night. She was upset over me and Sam."

"Well that is a feeling I know quite well. Should I talk to her?"

Amelia shook her head, "Nah, Sam has it. They are upstairs playing a game."

"Oh, well what are you doing, am I interrupting?"

Amelia smiled at her brother and tapped the chair next to her. "Come see, I am planning out Christmas dinner."

"Of course, you are. Let's plan for about thirty people. I think that's a good number."

"I was thinking forty so there will be left overs for each house."

Anthony nodded with approval, "That's a good idea too. This is why you do the planning." He picked up the paper she had been writing on and read over the lists. "You forgot one big thing."

"I did not!" She declared and snatched the paper from him and started reviewing the list. "It's all here, all the main dishes."

"Presents." He said that one word and it made Amelia smile. "You forgot presents, sister."

"Well I don't think I should have to plan out what everyone gets you bonehead."

"Mom used to shop for us, it was so easy." Antony's casual mention of their mom made them feel sad.

"She loved shopping."

"Yeah, it was her favorite part of Christmas, making us all happy."

Amelia let a few minutes of silence pass by while they sat there quietly. She broke the moment by saying, "Well we are just going to have to continue it without her, that will be how we keep her alive."

"I like that. Amy, I love you, and I'm sorry I don't tell you more."

She smiled and laughed, "I love you too Bub. Even if you are a bonehead."

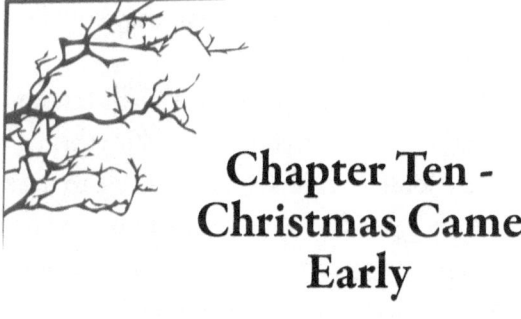

Chapter Ten -
Christmas Came
Early

AMELIA LOOKED THROUGH her list of items to do. With five days until Christmas she was getting anxious that there would be another disaster happen. The repairs from the hurricane had been completed. With the addition of Natalie to the community Anthony and John were able to fix everything they needed to in half of the time. Her group also included a wonderful woman named Jody who became the resident doctor. Amelia had taken her out to the library a couple times, so they could gather all the medical books possible. There was a smaller house in the middle of the communal that Amelia had used for community storage that was being converted into part of a doctor's office.

Their community was coming together slowly, it was working. She had her reservations about the eight new members but between Jody and Natalie it seemed like the group was hard working. They also had two children near Sunny's age, that gave Amelia hope that Sunny would come out of the shell she had locked herself into.

They had known she was still holding back. After the night of the outburst Amelia had tried to talk to Sunny but she was very blunt in saying she wasn't ready to talk. All they could do was hope that she would change her mind soon.

Amelia had taken John with her to the local Wal-Mart and borrowed all the pre-lighted trees she could find. With the help of the younger children, John and Natalie she was able to deck out the entire street with lighted trees. Natalie had helped her orchestrate electric supply by way of one of her solar powered generators that stored electricity. Tonight would be the un-veiling of the magical winter wonderland in Florida she had planned for everyone.

She had taken it to heart the idea that it was her responsi-bility to bring joy and happiness to all of the members of the community, so she held nothing back.

"Babe you ready to go?" Amelia glanced over at Sam and smiled.

"Sure am! Grabbing my notebook and I'll be right there!"

They were starting Christmas caroling tonight. She was well onto her way of being crowned the craziest woman left alive at the rate she was going with re-enactment.

"You know with all the stuff you did this year, next year will have to be even bigger to compare."

"Nah, think of this as a small town. What would a small town do? They would start a tradition. So, we will just carry this tradition on each year."

"If you say so! Come on woman you're making us late for your own shin-dig!"

"I'm coming, I'm coming!" She ran past him to the front door smiling, "Now who is late?"

The two of them walked down their sidewalk and stepped in front of the tent that they had put back up that they used at

Thanksgiving. Amelia's breath was caught in her throat. While she had been inside the house finishing up the menus someone had changed everything. The tent was decorated in white lights and flowers.

"What is going on?" She looked around and saw no one else but them standing there. "I thought we were all going to start singing tonight? Did they all back out?"

Sam grinned at Amelia and took her hand. "No, they are still going to come sing."

"Then where are they?"

He smirked at her, "You know what I love about you Amelia?"

She glanced at him then back around looking at everyone. "What did you do?" She inquired.

"I love that no matter how much you plan, no matter how smart you are, I can still surprise you every now and then."

Sam took a small velvet box out of his jacket pocket and placed his right knee on the ground. He opened the lid and a light pink gem sparkled back at her. "Amelia, I love you. Everyone here knows that. We don't know how long we have together but every second of that time I want to spend it with you by my side."

Amelia's voice caught in her throat, her hand went to cover her heart and tears formed in her eyes. "Sam..." She said softly.

"I know that you and I don't talk about the future much, but you're my future. I know it, you know it. Let's make it official. I want you forever to be mine."

"Oh Sam." She was crying now. She moved her head up and down as she walked to close the short distance between them.

She let him place the ring on her finger and smiled as he stood and took her hands in his.

"Is that a yes?" He inquired with a grinning smirk.

"It is. I still think we are way too young, but I do love you. I love you so much."

"I love you too. Now, how about a wedding?"

"What?" She let out a shout.

"Surprise!" She heard everyone in the community yell out at once and suddenly they all appeared out of nowhere.

Anthony walked up to her smiling. He pulled her in for a hug and held her close. "I promise I will kick his butt if he ever treats you badly. I am so happy for you two."

Amelia laughed at her brother's comments and hugged him back, "Why didn't you tell me?"

"What and ruin the surprise?" Anthony shook Sam's hand, "Guess we're really brothers now."

"Well may as well make it the truth since it's been that way for years."

"Where is Sunny?" Amelia looked around, and found her across the street talking to a boy. She raised her arm up and said, "Who is that?"

Anthony and Sam both looked in the direction she was pointing in. "That's Brody, Natalie's brother."

"Oh. Okay, let's leave her be for now."

Anthony hugged his sister again and then sent a signal over to Sarah. There was suddenly a string of music playing, that's when Amelia realized someone had found a way to pipe in music down into the tent.

"The waltz?" She chuckled at Sam. "What?"

"I thought you would want to have something formal and fancy for our day."

"Sam I am in jeans and a sweater we're not getting married right this second. I don't have the right outfit!"

"Excuse me, I believe we have that covered." Sarah said as her and Sunny walked over to her. "Sunny here found something she thinks you will like. Come with us."

Amelia couldn't believe what was happening. In the middle of the end of the world; she was getting married. An unplanned and unexpected wedding.

When they were alone Amelia grabbed Sunny's hand, "Sunny, I can't do this."

Sunny and Sarah smiled at her, "Yes you can," they both said.

"You love him Amelia." Sunny grinned at her.

"We hurt you though, how would this affect you?"

Sunny shook her head, "Amelia I'm sorry. I should have talked to you. I promise, I want this for you."

Amelia looked at Sarah, "What about you, I don't want you and Anthony really moving in together, I'll miss him terribly."

Sarah took Amelia by her shoulders, shook her a little, then looked at her square in the face. "Do you love him?"

"Yes."

"Then what else do you need Amy? Our world is dying, we don't know how much longer we have to live. Don't settle for the old ways. Empower yourself today."

"I just, this isn't what I pictured."

It was Sunny's turn to look at her with authority. "I have been hiding something from you. And I am ready to be honest."

Sarah and Amelia both looked down at Sunny. "Does she know about the rain?" Sunny asked.

"What rain?" Sarah questioned.

"I can control the weather, make it rain. It's kind of, well, I don't know. It's weird, but I can do it." Sunny felt brave as she spoke about her secret.

"How cool is that!" Sarah exclaimed. "Man, I wish I had some cool witchy powers, I'm totally jealous!"

"I can do more. I'm getting stronger the more I practice. Here." Sunny reached her hand into her pocket and pulled out a ring. "This was Sam's dads."

"How did you get this?" Amelia asked.

"I went to his house when he told me what he was planning."

"How? I didn't know anyone went back there." Sarah looked questioning at Sunny.

"I can sort of, transport myself places. That night I yelled at you I halfway went home. I was there in like shadow only my body was in my room, but my spirit wasn't. I was freaking out and that's when I fell and you all heard me crying."

"What?" Amelia and Sarah said together.

"And since then I've been practicing. Now I can poof places either as a full person or as a spirit. It's kinda cool. Anyway, I went to Sam's house and found the ring."

"But wasn't it on his dad?" Amelia asked.

Sunny looked up at her and smiled, "No, it was on his dresser. It's my wedding present for you both."

Sarah and Amelia gasped at the same time and all three girls hugged.

It was Sarah who spoke next, "You know us three are going to be family forever right. Because I am going to marry your brother. I'm not going to be foolish like you and deny the future. You will both be my sisters."

Amelia was crying now, holding the ring in her hand. "I love you both, I've always wanted sisters!"

The three of them took a few moments to cry and then Sarah spoke up. "It's my turn for surprises. Here you go." She walked over to a table and took the lid off of a box and pulled out a wedding dress.

"Oh, my word!" Amelia's voice was elevated in excitement.

"Natalie and I went into town, we found the most expensive dress possible. Do you like it?"

"It's perfect!" Amelia ran her hands over it and cried some more. "I need to shower." All three girls laughed and nodded together. "I can't get married all dirty. You have to tell him to postpone it for at least two hours."

Sam came walking around the corner smiling like the Cheshire Cat. "I'll give you one hour and I'm timing you, go!"

Amelia grinned at him and then quickly nodded to the other ladies and they all ran towards her house.

Anthony looked at his sister as she ran towards the house with the other two ladies in his world that completed his family.

"Somehow we have found a way to be blessed during this time." He said to Sam.

"Yeah, I don't know how we would have all survived without one another."

Natalie and John walked up together laughing and smiled at them. "Big night for you two. Gaining a wife and brother."

Natalie seemed to have become a member of their community relatively easily. It almost was as if she had been there from the start.

"It's a day I wish we could record somehow."

Natalie grinned and said, "Ah hah, I have a wedding present for the groom." She reached into the bag she was carrying and pulled out a Polaroid camera. "Happy wedding day!"

Anthony looked at Sam's face and saw the happiness in his eyes. This was truly a day to rejoice. The end hadn't won, hadn't defeated them.

"Thank you, Natalie, I don't know what to say."

"You don't need to say anything, you got me water that first night we were here. Call it even. Hope you two have lots of happiness!"

Anthony watched as Sam hugged Natalie. He was happy for his best friend. But it was hard for him to think of his sister belonging to him, someone else. She and he had been through life together from the start, he didn't want to think of her seeking out someone else for help.

But then he realized for the last year and a half she already had. Even before they were officially dating. They had been floating together while they were in school too. It was as if the shock was hitting him all over again, he wished Sarah was with him.

Sarah. She brought him such easy peace inside his chaotic mind.

"Man, you okay?" Sam said to him.

"Yeah, just thinking of my sister. It's going to be weird."

"But not a bad weird I hope, I mean we've known each other for our whole lives. Nothing is going to change."

"Well one big thing will change." John said while laughing and winking at Natalie.

"Oh man don't say that, it's my sister!" Anthony protested.

Sam's face had his classic grin back. "I know, I can't wait."

"Don't make me beat your ass right here before you actually get married."

"Nah, I promise to be a gentleman."

Natalie was the first to burst into laughter and they all eventually let it blow over. "In light of this new development, how about I let you know that I suggested to Sunny to spend the night over at Anthony and Sarah's. I would take her with me, but I think her, and Brody, are flirting and I'm not okay with that just yet."

Sam nodded in agreement, "Yeah me too, def not ready for all that yet."

"I think Sarah already planned for that actually, because she was making up a guest bed and I wasn't sure why. Makes sense now." Anthony had begun openly glaring at Sam now.

"Look man you're the one who told me to go ahead with this you can't get mad at me, we're all adults you know!"

John stepped in between the two of them teasingly. "Boys do I need to separate you."

"I'm fine man, I just, it's my sister, I love her. I want her safe."

"I know Anthony, I love her too. I'll keep her safe."

While they were all talking the other ladies of the community had brought out food and plates. They were setting everything up as nice as it could be and Anthony realized they weren't dressed. "Dude, we need to change."

Sam looked down and nodded, "Yeah we do. See y'all soon. Wedding starts in 30."

AS AMELIA STEPPED OUT of her house Anthony was there waiting for her with his arm extended out. "May I escort, my beautiful sister, to her groom?"

"Oh Anthony." She sniffled and nodded, "Yes of course."

They walked along the concrete path, the sun had begun to fade, and someone had lighted up all the trees. The street looked perfect, white iced trees illuminated each driveway and the tent had the lgihts set up. She was getting married by candle light, she saw at least fifty handles displayed.

"It's so perfect."

"Only the best for the number one woman in my life."

"Sarah's sliding into that spot Bub."

"No, no one will replace you twin."

"Sam's not replacing you either Anthony."

As she set foot into the tent she heard the music start. Everyone stood and looked back at her. She saw Sunny standing next to Sarah, both holding flowers. They had given Amelia her bouquet after she came out of the shower. Sam was wearing a light gray suit and a tie that matched the ring. He was the most handsome person she had ever seen. John was standing in the middle between Sunny and Sam. She had decided Sunny should be the maid of honor and assumed John was doing the service.

"You're not going to marry me?" She asked Anthony.

"Someone has to give you away. That's my job. Mom and Dad would be proud of everything you've done here. I have to represent them."

They started their walk down the aisle and she felt the tears start again. She did her best to hold them in. When they reached Sam, everyone sat down behind her. Anthony placed her hand in Sam's and grinned at her.

John started, "Who here gives this woman a way."

"I do," Anthony spoke with confidence, that warmed Amelia down to the core of her bones.

Sam and Anthony shook hands, then Anthony went to sit down on the left side of the audience.

"We're gathered today to join in union Sam and Amelia. But it is more than that. It's the start of the continuation of our world. Their first to carry the torches our parents passed onto us. They're our beacon of hope. Together, along with their family and friends, they will help our community survive past this year and into many more to come."

As John spoke Amelia couldn't stop focusing on the ring in her hand and how Sunny acquired it. So much was changing, nothing was the same as it was two months ago, six months ago or two years ago, before all of this happened. As she felt her heart start to race she heard John call her name.

"Amelia, do you take Sam Martin to be your husband? To have and to hold, for better or worse, sickness or health, in the apocalypse or normal life, zombies and all, as long as you both shall live?"

Amelia grinned up at Sam, "I do."

"And Sam, do you take Amelia Kay to be your wife? To have and to hold, for better or worse, sickness or health, in the apocalypse or normal life, zombies and all, as long as you both shall live?"

Sam stepped closer, "Without a doubt, I do."

"The rings please." John reached his hand out and they both placed their rings in his hand. After he made the sign of the cross and said a small blessing over them he said, "Each of you take your ring and place it on your partner's finger and repeat after me."

They both reached for their rings simultaneously and waited for the instructions.

"This ring is a symbol of my love and affection to you. May you always wear it, and may it provide you protection for all of our lives."

They repeated the lines, and both were grinning at one another.

"By the power vested in me by Mr. Anthony Davis I now declare you Mr. and Mrs. Wells. You may kiss your bride."

They leaned into one another, as he kissed her, all the worries and trepidation's she had felt just moments ago vanished. This was the right choice. This was love. She heard everyone around them start to clap, she managed to tune it all out. She was married, and this was the man she wanted forever.

Before she had a chance to say anything he leaned over and scooped her up in his arms and spun her around. She heard someone call out, "Smile!" Sam turned them towards Natalie and we both smiled. She captured a picture of them, a picture. Amelia started to cry. It was the perfect wedding and there were pictures. This was truly her day, a day she could have forever.

"Thank you, Sam. This was great."

"It was my pleasure to give this to you. You work so hard for everyone else. We all wanted you to have something that was just yours. Now come on, let's take more pictures and eat. I'm starved!"

Chapter Eleven -
Testing Boundaries

WHEN PEOPLE READ ABOUT the apocalyptic stories in the past, it never occurred to anyone to discuss how they went from 'the world is coming to an end' to 'survival'. This is what Sunny was having complications with, and what caused her to seek out more and more books about dystopian literature. It began to worry Sam, she was spending all her time over the last two months reading. Whether it was *The Hunger Games*, *Divergent* or *1984* she was trying too hard. Sam wanted her to have more fun, but he feared that since the wedding she had withdrawn further inside herself and now he didn't know what to do about it.

Without much thought about his actions he walked into Sunny's room one day when she was out with Amelia. He had wanted to take the opportunity to see what she had been doing with all her time alone in her room besides reading. At first, he hadn't noticed anything wrong, when he looked closer at her dresser he saw a book. A book that he knew he had seen before but didn't know from where. When he walked closer to it he got a feeling in his gut that told him something wasn't okay.

He reached his arm out and let his fingers trace over the cover. Something that felt like electricity shot through his arm and it made him jump backwards. Sam shook his arm out, rubbed the muscles. He was more curious now, how could a book sitting on a dresser hold static electricity like that. He reached his arm back out and this time instead of tracing the cover he opened it. The first page said family bible. That's where he had seen it, at his grandparent's house before. As he started to turn the pages he realized this wasn't a traditional family bible, it was something, more devious.

Sam let his curiosity get the better of him and he continued thumbing through the pages of the leather-bound book. It was calling to him, he felt it in his bones. Something was compelling him to keep looking. It wasn't until he stepped back from the dresser and let his eyes focus on something else that he realized the pages he read out of the book weren't written in English. After rubbing his eyes and blinking a lot he looked back at the text and guessed it was some form of Arabic.

"Why did my grandparents have this?" He said out loud to no one.

He closed the book and stepped out of his cousin's room and shut the door as if he wasn't in there. What was she up to? They had known she was controlling the weather, but he had never taken the time to analyze what else she may be doing. How had she even gotten that book into her room? As far as he knew no one had taken her to her home, let alone their grandparents place. Something wasn't sitting right with him over this.

"Sam, we're home!" He heard Amelia's voice call out from downstairs. His wife, he couldn't stop smiling every time he said that, his wife's voice always made him feel good.

"Hey my favorite ladies!" He called to them as he traveled down the stairs and greeted them in the foyer. "How was shopping?"

"You know it wasn't like real shopping Sam." Sunny teased him.

"Let's see, was it at a mall?" He asked.

"Yes." Sunny replied.

"Did you use bags and lots of them?" He grinned, looking at the bags they each held in their clutches.

"Duh." Sunny rolled her eyes as she lifted her arms up.

"Then I say, if it looks like a duck, quack's like a duck,"

Sunny interrupted him, "I know, it's a duck." She started to walk upstairs as she shook her head. "Sometimes I worry about you Sam."

He didn't respond to her, but he did look over Amelia and grinned at her, "Did you break the bank?"

Amelia gave him a toothy smile and said, "Well I broke a nail, does that count?"

Sam leaned over and kissed her lips softly then took a few of the bags off her arms. "I'll help you put all these away. What did you get? It feels like bricks, these are so heavy."

"Our little community is growing, so I have been working up an idea."

"Oh boy, this sounds like more work."

"It will be, but worth it in the end I think. Here let me show you." Amelia took one of the bags from him and walked over to the couch and displayed the contents. "See, people are growing in size right, and we can't all just keep wearing hand-me-downs. Eventually they will be just tattered rags. So, I am going to start shopping every day for a month and collect items. We have room in the pantry house with the doctor's office that we can also have a make shift store."

She pulled more items out of more bags, "This way people can 'shop' when they need something instead of always having to bum a way to the mall or some store."

"How are you going to keep people from hoarding and taking all of them?" Sam asked.

"Well I thought about that too. Since money isn't really any good we can issue rations."

"Like we do the water?" He asked.

Amelia motioned with her head, "Yep, let's say at first everyone can have three clothing outfits and seven pairs of underwear and socks."

"Why three and seven?"

"Here's my logic Sam. First, well, we all kinda have clothes now so it isn't like we're destitute. But I bet people need new underwear, I know you do."

"Hey!" He protested.

She waved him away, "So then after the first month we can move it to one outfit and two underwear each month per person. I'll of course need to keep going to the stores and gathering as much clothing as I can. There is an Old Navy a ways down I want to hit up too."

"Let me guess, you're going to manage all of this, right?"

"Of course." She said without hesitation.

"Don't you think that you are kinda doing enough as it is?"

"Well I thought about that too, and I think this would be a good task for Sarah and me to do with Sunny. It will give her some purpose, some responsibility. Like she can manage displaying everything and refilling shelves when product gets low.

Sarah and I can do the bookkeeping. We can take turns and the store could maybe only be open two days a week or something simple at first."

"Have you talked to your brother about this?"

"Sure, we talked about it in passing before, but I haven't told him we were going through with anything just yet. I was leaving that for Sarah to do. Since he is practically living over there full time, she sees him more than I do now days."

"Well, okay. It isn't like I can tell you no, but I don't want you doing any more projects. We need to focus on the ones we currently have. We still have our family farm to tend, our community farm to tend and all of our regular household chores."

"Sam, it isn't like I don't know all this. You remember who it is that manages things on a daily basis, right?"

"You're right, let's not fight. I just, I don't want you overworked." Sam squeezed Amelia's hand and gave her a smile. "You're such an amazing woman, you want to do so much. I just want to look out for you that's all."

The two of them sat there on the couch holding hands for a few moments before the silence was broken by a loud explosion.

"What was that?" Amelia exclaimed, before the both raced upstairs to check on Sunny.

For the second time that day Sam walked into Sunny's private space without permission, except this time he didn't need to sneak around to see the problem. There was his baby cousin, sitting on the floor, with black soot all over her face and a cauldron on the floor in front of her.

"What in the hell are you doing Sunny?" Sam barked out.

"Clearly I am blowing myself up Sam." She snapped right back at him.

"Don't take that attitude with me Sunny I saw that book I know you're up to something, you're hiding it from me and I'm not okay with that." Sam reached down and put his hand around Sunny's arm and pulled her into a standing position. "Spill it Sunny, what is going on?"

"What do you mean you know about the book, were you in my room?" Sunny shouted at her cousin.

"I mean that yeah I was and you're my responsibility. I knew something was up and I needed to see what it was."

"You had no right Sam, no right! None! This is my room. You can't just come in here whenever you want."

"Sunny, stop you need to explain how you got to our grandparent's house without help."

"Sam, maybe you shouldn't yell at Sunny, this isn't helping anything." Amelia came around to Sunny's side and put an arm about her shoulders. "Sweetie, I think you need to tell him what's going on."

He looked over at his wife and felt his blood start to boil, "Amelia, you know what's going on?"

She nodded, and Sam glared at his cousin. "Spill it Sunny."

Sunny's eyes were full of tears and he could see the streaks they were starting to cause on her soot stained face. "Sam you know something's wrong with me."

"I don't think anything is wrong with you." He saw his cousin grab his wife's hand.

"Yes, something is, I'm different. And that book over there is helping me."

"I felt something weird when I was reading the book, what kind of family bible is it?"

"You could read it too?" Amelia questioned.

"Yeah, but I don't know how, it's in Arabic."

Sunny's head moved up and down, "Yeah I can read it, but Amelia can't. She doesn't have the gift. From what I can tell it's genetic."

"What is Sunny?"

"The power. I'm a witch." She started to sniffle her nose and he saw Amelia pull her in closer, he felt horrible for how he was handling this.

"Amelia, you should have told me."

"I promised Sunny I would let her do it. I didn't know that you were touched with it too."

Sam felt his head starting to spin. He walked over to Sunny's bed and sat down on the edge. "This seems like a lot to take in, can you just start from the beginning please."

Over the course of an hour Sunny explained about her ability to teleport spiritually to other locations. How she had started to work spells she had found in their family bible. He stayed quiet through her explanation of how she realized her powers were more than what he had thought controlling the weather was.

"Sam are you okay?" Amelia asked her husband as she walked into their room.

"Not really, Sunny told me a lot of things I just can't be-lieve." Sam was sitting in the bed writing down what Sunny had explained to him. "Did you know about all of this?"

She shook her head back and forth, "No, not about all the genetic stuff, but I did know her powers were strengthening."

"It's still confusing, you know I didn't do great at the genet-ics portion in science class."

"It was pretty simple Sam. She said your grandparent's book said it was a recessive gene."

"Yeah but I don't get that Amelia, how can she have this stuff and her parents didn't."

"Sam don't you remember when Mrs. Alberta taught us the Punnett Squares?"

"No, not at all."

"Well Sunny said your grandma was a witch and your grandpa was not. Too bad she is gone we could have asked her lots of questions."

"Yeah but how is Sunny a witch and I'm not?"

"Your grandma would have passed on a witch gene to both of her sons. I guess it would have to come from the mom's too, to be a witch. Sunny's mom must have either been a witch or had the recessive gene too."

"So, what my mom then didn't?"

"If she did have the gene there was only a fifty percent chance of her passing it to you. Those aren't the greatest odds you know."

Sam rubbed his head, "This is giving me a headache. Let's just go to bed and we can deal with it in the morning."

He kept his head on his pillow for hours, thinking about Sunny. At first he was furious at both her and Amelia for keeping this from him. From Anthony too. They had been a team from the start of the event, and built this community into what it had become. Sam kept thinking about the hurricane and the damage it caused. Did Sunny make that happen, or make it worse?

What if she lost control and more damage was done.

Sam sat up from his bed and swung his feet over the edge and lightly pressed his feet to the floor. He wanted to make sure he didn't disturb Amelia and wake her up. Using the tips of his toes, he made his way down the hallway and downstairs. He crossed through the living room and into the kitchen, he was shocked to see Anthony sitting at the table.

"Hey man, thought you would be over at Sarah's."

"Yeah, we had a fight, so I came home." Anthony's face showed his pain and Sam felt for him.

"Want to talk about it?" Sam stretched his arm into the re-frigerator and pulled out the pitcher of iced tea and poured himself a drink.

Shrugging Anthony responded, "I don't know. Sure. She wants us to get married next."

"We all thought you would be next" Sam said as he sat down across from his brother-in-law.

"That's just it, everyone assumes it and I just don't want to." Anthony took a gulp from his glass and swiped his hand over his lips. "I just don't feel ready."

"But you practically live with her now."

"Yeah, but I can still come home. We aren't you and Amelia, you two have known each other practically our whole lives."

Sam indicated yes with his head, "Yeah but if you're not ready then you're not ready. You can't do everything the same as your sister and I."

"That's what I told Sarah and she didn't like it."

"Did you ask her why marriage is so important to her?"

Anthony nodded, "Yeah, because she says it's the end of the world and we could die tomorrow so she wants to make the most of it."

Sam couldn't fault the logic there, he felt the same way. "Want me to take your mind off of your love drama?"

"Not if you're going to tell me about you and my sister drama."

"Ha! Your sister and I are perfect we don't have any drama. No, I was going to update you on Sunny drama."

"Is she okay?" Anthony perked up, his voice layered in concern.

"She is fine if that is what you're asking. You know how she can control the weather?"

"Yes..." Anthony said with a slight hesitation.

"As it turns out she can do more than that, or rather, is working towards doing a lot more than that. She is a full-blown witch."

"Really? Are you sure?"

Sam took another drink of his iced tea, "Yeah, she has these abilities that our grandmother apparently had. I never knew about it. Amelia has known for a while."

"What kind of abilities, like can she turn people to toads?"

Sam laughed, "I am pretty sure that is strictly a movie thing. But she can astral project, she is working on spells and her ability with the weather is getting stronger."

"Wow, I have to say I didn't see that coming. When did you find out that her powers had increased so dramatically?"

"Tonight, and I am not quite sure when your sister found out." Sam took another drink and then stood from the table. "Anthony, for what it's worth I really do think Sarah is right. Go home to her. You love her and there are far scarier things than living with the woman you love. If you're not ready for marriage then just move in with her. You know you can always come back here anytime you decide it isn't right."

"Maybe Sam, I'll think on it tonight and talk to her tomorrow."

"Goodnight Anthony, see you in the morning."

Sam walked out of the kitchen and made his way back to his room upstairs. He wasn't going to let the witch issue bother him tonight, there is always tomorrow to dwell. Tonight, he wanted to go and be with Amelia, and that was what he was going to do.

Chapter Twelve - Coming To Terms

THE NEXT FEW WEEKS were spent with the women working on the new clothing shop and Anthony working on training. Sunny had a dream that had spooked him and Sam, and he didn't want to risk her new powers not including her being clairvoyant with the abilities to see possible futures.

Sunny had painted a picture about a rainy night in the next year sometime where their walls were being attacked by strangers. Their community had fallen, and everyone was kicked out by the invading colony of survivors. What really had him perplexed was how Sunny had described the leader. A well-built man with silver hair and a staff. Anthony didn't know what to do what that. Who used a staff other than the elderly? Sunny said that the man didn't seem too much older than them, but he wasn't sure he believed it. The way she said silver hair didn't give him the warm and fuzzies. But it did make him want to prepare in case her dream was true.

Over these few weeks Anthony had gone out with John and Sam a dozen times to start procuring weapons. The women weren't in favor of this, they worried the younger kids would find a way to get ahold of them. Anthony was convinced that sooner or later, even if it wasn't in the way of Sunny's dream went, they would be attacked. It was common awareness that this community wasn't the only one to survive since the stores continued to lose supplies outside of what they were taking. It was inevitable that someone eventually would try and take away what was theirs.

Another source of concern had been their modes of transportation. Their last vehicle was on its last gallon of fuel and they hadn't found a gas station to replenish the fuel close to home in a while. Another reason to believe that there were more survivors, the gasoline was gone. Amelia had suggested they use animals. At the time, Anthony had ignored her suggestion saying that it wasn't the seventeenth century, but he was now realizing horse powered fuel would be better than the alternative.

Finding ways to make all these different issues from coming to life and solve them was a lot of pressure, and it was starting to weigh heavily on him. After he talked with Sam about the whole idea of marriage, his feelings of eternity seemed to lessen with dread. Instead, what had replaced it were loads of responsibility. He was having to come to terms with certain situations that he wasn't okay with.

For instance, worrying about their community following common rules.

In his last school year, he had been learning about different governments. While he had an 'a' in the class, he hadn't paid enough attention to some of the different philosophers that his teacher was trying to instruct on. He remembered the obvious John Locke and his social contract, but he couldn't remember everything that had gone into it. He had brought it up to Sarah one day at dinner and she suggested that they go to the library and see what they could find.

Anthony wanted to make sure that everyone felt he was being fair with the rules that everyone had agreed upon, but he was well aware that their community had gone from just four people to over twenty. As time continued it was obvious there would be more. Their houses inside the subdivision would easily hold at least five more families comfortably. There had been talk of converting one of the houses into more of an apartment home with a shared kitchen area to accommodate people who weren't here with families but still wanted a central community of people. A lot had changed in a year. Anthony just wanted the community to adapt and continue to thrive.

"I've been watching you sit at your desk now for over an hour and I haven't seen you do anything." Sarah said as she walked past him holding a basket of laundry.

With a shrug he responded, "I'm doing stuff you just can't tell."

"I don't think that pondering the world's problems counts as productive."

"Of course it does, when you're coming up with more ways for the community to keep growing."

"What do you have in mind?" She had set the basket down on the living room floor and took a spot next to it on the couch and started pulling out each piece of clothing one by one to fold.

"Well, for instance, I think I was wrong and we should try to find livestock to use as transportation."

"Does your sister know you just said that? Her head may explode!" Sarah was laughing as she spoke. The sound of her voice always made him feel calm, and even when she was teasing him, he still enjoyed it.

"I haven't told her yet, I was waiting for her birthday." Anthony pulled some paper out of his desk and grabbed his pen. He started writing some items down on the lined papers and tried to focus hard on the importance of priorities and what issues need to be solved first.

"What else is bothering you?" Sarah was holding up his boxers and started laughing, "I think you need to go shopping, is that on your list, these have a huge hole in them."

"It's on my list, right under, I don't know, shower and shave. Very important. I'll go to our little store tomorrow, I promise."

"I have our vouchers for clothing on the fridge in the kitchen, you just need to take it with you."

"You don't really think I will need that do you? It's my sister!"

Sarah shook her head, "It's Sunny, and she is hard pressed to give anyone a break. I'll bet that her books are as meticulous as the old accountants were before the incident happened."

"Lovely. Well I guess three pairs of boxers it is."

"You know Anthony, your sister is really doing a great job, and she is finding the needs of the community, and almost tricking everyone into fixing the issues before they become a problem."

"Do you not think I am doing a good job too?" Anthony set his paper aside and looked at her, his attention zoned in on her.

"It isn't that you aren't doing a good job, you both are. It is just different approaches, that's all."

"I think we need rules, like legit laws." He had shuffled more paper around and started writing down on the paper again. "With consequences.

"How do you think you will get everyone's buy in?

"What do you mean by everyone's? I am in charge here, I made that known before anyone new moved in." He was now staring right at Sarah and he watched her look away and avoid his eye contact. "Why, Sarah what have you heard?"

"It isn't a big deal, I just heard that you're a little too uptight on some things and that Amelia should be in charge."

"That isn't going to happen, she is too busy, Sam wouldn't tolerate it."

"What do you mean, tolerate? Sam doesn't have a say in everything she does. You can't tell me what to do all the time."

Anthony ran his hands over his face and through his hair. He dropped his head back to the chair and looked up to the ceiling, "I don't know Sarah maybe I am saying this wrong."

"So, try again Anthony."

"What I mean is, we all live in a social contract of some kind. In our community we offer food, water, clothing and pro-tection in exchange for man hours worked and decent behavior towards each other."

"Right, and have you thought about what would happen if someone doesn't follow those rules?"

"That's what I have been spending the last hour thinking about. We all have to come to terms that things have changed and are never going back to the way they were. We have to ac-cept that. So, given that constraint it is time we made actual laws for us all to follow."

"Don't we still have the laws of the United States?"

"Sarah, we don't even know if the country is still a country, or if it is just made up of teenagers wandering around. Do you even remember when the last time you saw an adult?"

She didn't respond with anything she just sat there folding more laundry. He could tell she was thinking but didn't speak. He was going to let her come to the same conclusions he had come to earlier in the day. "Okay, so what are you suggesting?"

"We go old school."

"What like Moses and the burning bush?" She smiled at him and that made Anthony start to laugh.

"No goof, I said old school not biblical." He took his finger and tapped his brain, "Remember how we were looking up philosophers, well I mean old school. Like John Locke. The whole social contract. We make one, well we have one, we just need to write it down and enforce it if anything ever happens.

"Oh, well, okay I think that could work, once you run it past the community."

Anthony stood up and walked over to Sarah, he sat down next to her and started folding some of the clothing she hadn't got to yet. "Here is my idea on that. You know how the Native Americans had tribal councils?"

"Not really, but let's pretend I know what you're talking about."

"Well they didn't just have a chief they had a council of advisors to the chief. I think we need that."

"So, you want to be chief and you want others serving you with advice."

Anthony nodded, "Yes, exactly."

Sarah shook her head back and forth, "Nope that won't' work."

"Why won't it?"

"Because no one voted for you, they will feel resentment if they are forced to follow someone as a leader. You need to have an election."

"An election! So, fifteen out of twenty-seven people can run for office and everyone can have one or two votes! No way, that isn't going to happen.

"So, then what if you have a tribunal? You know it can be the top three people. Maybe then it won't feel so one sided. Everyone has a voice. Like elections."

"I don't want elections right now at this point I think we need directions. But I do like the idea of three solid leaders."

"You realize it can't be you, Amelia and Sam, right?" Sarah stated.

"And why not?"

"Because it isn't representative. It would need to be one person per family. So, it would be either you, Sam or Amelia but only one since you are all in the same family now."

"I guess, I'll have to think about it. But let me tell you what really has been worrying me for the immediate future and why I think we need to start stock piling guns."

Sarah's facial expression was clearly in shock. She listened quietly as Anthony explained everything Sunny had predicted and why it was bothering him so greatly. After he had finished going into the details that Amelia had explained to him about witches he thought Sarah would laugh at him and call him crazy. Instead she wrapped her arms around him and kissed him.

"Thank you, Anthony, thank you for wanting to do this job to protect us."

"Of course, I love you Sarah."

"No, I don't just mean me, I mean the community. I know it is a thankless job, so I am thanking you."

"Just one of the many reasons I love you." Anthony leaned into her and gave her a soft kiss on the lips. "I love you with all my heart."

"Then why do you run away when I mention us getting married."

"You mean aside from the fact we are still teenagers?"

"Anthony! Don't make this about age."

He placed his palm against her cheek, "I know it isn't a joke or about age. I'm just anxious about it. I just, I don't want to make any mistakes or do anything wrong."

"We are going to make mistakes, there is so much we don't know, but we can't always hide just because we are scared. We have to face it head on."

"It is obvious you're right, but I don't know how to do that, I don't know how to be like you."

"That's why we are partners, so when you fall short, I can get you across the finish line."

"So, what are you wanting a big ceremony like we gave my sister?"

She shook her head no, "I just want you and me, and maybe the little family we have."

"I am not ready for babies." Anthony said.

"Neither am I, just want you. I want you and me."

"Okay."

"What?" Sarah asked with a pitch of excitement in her voice. "Did you just say yes?"

"I did not, I said, 'okay.' Which means," Anthony turned his whole body to face Sarah and had her sitting down in the couch with her back against the back of the sofa. "Sarah will you become Mrs. Davis?"

"Tell me something, does marrying you mean I get special privileges in breaking the rules?" She teased.

"Depends on the rule, I may have to give you a special punishment though, we'll just have to see."

Sarah's face lighted up, her smile was ear to ear. "Yes Anthony, yes I will marry you."

He leaned into her and kissed her. At first it was soft but then it became fiercer. He did love her, and he did want her. His fears were just that, fears, and he needed to find a way to push those aside.

"Stop thinking Anthony and just kiss me."

"Yes ma'am."

After spending the evening celebrating just the two of them Anthony went out into the community with a new jaunt to his step. He surprised himself by feeling excited, but he didn't want to jinx it so he just didn't think about it. Today was Thursday and everyone had their vegetable reporting due on Thursday, so he knew he could find most of the heads of each house in the vegetable homestead. Which, of course, was ran by his sister.

Walking into the room he looked around to see who all had shown up on time for their delivery and reports. He sauntered in past a couple people and took his seat that had been assigned to him since the start of the community vegetable reporting. Each house had a seat at the table. After everyone arrived and some general conversation had subsided he decided to call the meeting to order.

"Everyone, I want to thank you for coming today. Before we get on with our weekly reporting I think updating all of you on some issues I have discovered is most prudent."

"What's going on Anthony?" Sam asked from his left. Since he had moved out of the house Amelia had let Sam take over in representing their house in the meetings. She felt he was best suited for the role and Sam loved it.

"I have been assessing our assets and our buildings, it occurs to me that if we were ever under attack that we would be ill prepared. I think we need to start hunting parties for livestock, like horses, and guns."

Everyone in the room was a man except for Natalie. He hadn't anticipated any backlash from Natalie or he guys. Sam raised his eyes and looked straight at Anthony. They mentally shared the same thought about Sunny and Anthony nodded at his lifelong friend.

"I think it's long overdue." Natalie said.

Someone else seconded her comment and within five minutes they had worked out a schedule for 'hunting parties' to focus on ammunition and guns to bring to the community.

"While we are on the planning topic there is one more thing I want to bring up. Since we are essentially the leaders of the community I felt it was best to bring it up here first."

It was John's turn to look over and question Anthony, "There is more?"

"This one isn't an imminent threat, it is more of a, how do I put this, future for our little colony. Have you all heard of John Locke?"

"The philosopher from government class?" Sam asked.

"Yep one in the same." Anthony went into his idea about the social contract and his idea about the governing body. After a few minutes of silence with no one talking he had the thought that maybe he had pushed it too far. Then someone spoke up.

"You're right, we need this. But I don't know if I like the idea of a tribunal." Natalie said.

"Why not, it seems fair, there won't be any tiebreakers on issues. Could be like our own little government." Anthony had promised Sarah he wouldn't be defensive if someone didn't agree with him, but he was struggling with it. He felt very defensive.

"Because what if people try to bribe one another?" She questioned.

"There would have to be clear moral and ethical rules that must be followed when being in the leadership role. And that isn't saying there aren't other places for more leaders. I just think if we had clear direction on the foundation it will help us grow."

"Are we taking in more people?" John asked.

"Not that I know of, but that will change in the future it's bound to."

"Let's do it." Sam declared confidently.

Natalie looked around the room, "So pretty much the people who will make up the tribunal are in this room, except for Amelia."

"She can't be on it." Anthony said quickly which caused Sam to turn his head and look defensive for his wife. "She and I are family only one of us can be."

"Amelia is my family now, not yours."

Anthony shook his head at his brother-in-law, "We are family too. Only one of us can be on there."

"What about Sarah?" Sam retorted with.

"What about her?"

"Are you planning on marrying her?" Sam's stare was dead set on Anthony's face, it was almost as if he was taking a laser beam and slicing his face in half.

"I am .... But not right this exact minute."

"Whoa, so now you and I are going to be related too?" John said holding his hands up.

"Didn't this just get interesting?" Natalie said laughing.

Others in the room began talking and now no one could hear anything going on.

"Guys come on." Anthony tried getting peoples' attention. He finally had to resort to yelling, "STOP!" When everyone silenced their voices, he continued. "Okay so clearly there are some logistical issues on who will lead but we all agree overall, we need to put some type of social contract into place, right?"

Everyone nodded and agreed to table the topic until after they all had the chance to think about it on their own. After the meeting was over Sam walked over to Anthony and pulled him into a corner where no one could hear them.

"It's a good thing we're going to start getting weapons, Sunny had another dream and this one was more specific. The guy is coming, and we know his name, Laken."

Chapter Thirteen -
He Who Casts
Stones

SAM STARTED PACING up and down the hallway while Sunny explained to Anthony her latest dream. He had listened closely the first time she told it, and the idea of her knowing this strange guy's name bothered him. How had her powers grown to such a point that she could detect names? What really got under his skin was that she was able to do all of this and he couldn't do anything. Amelia kept wondering how many other people were able to do stuff similar to this. She also was certain there must be others in the community who could. She didn't think Sunny was the only one.

What they didn't know was how to determine if this was a truth or just a hopeful thought. Amelia wanted to speak with each of the families' one on one to discuss what Sunny could do, see if others could as well. Sam was concerned that would cause ridicule towards his cousin and that he wasn't willing to risk.

Anthony walked out of Sunny's room, Sam could see his friend was stressed out. Anthony had his right hand running over his face and through his hair, he always carried the weight of the world on his shoulders, and this new development wasn't any different.

"It's all crazy right?" Sam walked over and put his hand on his friends' shoulder. He knew what he was feeling because Sam and Amelia were experiencing it too. Sunny and her powers were a lot to take in and it made everything harder knowing that conventional beliefs didn't support any of it.

"She says there are two main guys heading straight for us. Sunny thinks we have two months max to prepare."

Sam gestured with his head, "Yeah and that there was about twenty-five of them too, she said there are adults with them."

"Actually, she said the leader, Laken, and his second-in-command, Collins, she believes are adults. That half of the people with them are adults and that they have vehicles."

Shaking his head back and forth, Sam sighed out loud. "How can she possibly know any of this?"

Anthony shrugged his shoulders, "Who knows but she does. And while I am not completely convinced that she is right, she had enough details that make me believe her. We have got to start preparing."

"Amelia wants us to tell the group about Sunny and see if anyone else has abilities too." Sam's stomach churned as he said the sentence, he felt deep inside that doing that would cause more problems than it would help.

"Sam, she's right, the people have a right to know how we know all of this."

"But what will they do to Sunny? I can't have everyone hating her or being scared of her."

Amelia stepped out of Sunny's room just then and said, "I have an idea about that, why do we have to give them Sunny's name? Why can't we just tell them we have someone who can do this, and they are helping us? We don't have to be so specific that we give Sunny away like that."

Anthony moved his shoulders up and down again, "I don't know sis, and I don't know these people well enough if they will just take our word without any proof."

Sam's head turned towards Sunny's door, "What kind of proof do you think they will want?"

Anthony said without missing a beat, "If I were them I would want to see her perform something."

"Great so we are going to make a freak show out of her, parade her around like some sort of act people can pay admission to. No, I don't think so." Sam said boldly. His arms were crossed over his chest and he was standing protectively in front of Sunny's door.

"I didn't say we would make her a freak show, Sam." Anthony retorted.

"That's exactly what would happen if we told them what you're saying we should tell them. I can't do that."

"Sam, stop." Sunny's voice came from behind him. All of the adults turned to look at the young witch. "I want to do it. I want to do what Amelia suggests."

His heart broke as he looked at his cousin. He knelt down and looked her square in the eye. "Sunny you don't have to do that, you can stay behind the scenes with just us."

Her hand reached out to touch his hand, "Sam I love you, and I know you're protecting me. But I can handle it."

"What if people start to hate you for being different?" Sam held his cousin's hands in his own, looking into her innocent eyes.

"Then they hate me. But what if they believe me and it protects all of us? It isn't just the four of us, it's everyone." Sunny looked over at Amelia, "I was jealous of her, I hated that she took my only family member away from me. But you made me give her a chance. And now I have a sister." Sunny leaned into Sam and wrapped her arms around his neck and held him with all her might. "I have to do this Sam. We have to do this. To save everyone. To save your future, my future. We have to."

"Sunny is very wise beyond her years." Amelia said in a low toned voice.

Anthony nodded his head in agreement with his sister, "Sam, we need to let the girls do this."

"No matter what you're my family and I will always want to protect you, Sunny," Sam wiped a tear from his eye as he looked at her. "But okay, I will support this. So long as either Anthony or I are with you both when you tell people, you have to promise me that."

"Deal." Sunny smiled and hugged Sam again. The two of them stayed embracing for a few minutes before Sunny laid the next bomb down. "Laken is the leader, but his son Collins, he is the one who killed everyone."

John and Sarah had finally had a few minutes to themselves. Today at the weekly meeting had left John uneasy with Anthony's comment about marriage. He wanted to see or rather hear for himself from his sister on what was going on between the two of them. He had walked straight to her house after everyone departed the garden production meeting.

"John, I don't know why you are so worried." Sarah handed him a cup of tea and they were sitting in the living room together. The awkward tension in the room was making it harder for him to feel safe in talking about something that could potentially cause any problems.

"I am worried because we don't really know them that well. It hasn't been very long."

"What are you afraid we don't know? You supported Sam and Amelia getting married."

"That's totally different Sarah, Amelia wasn't my sister. And they all grew up together. We are not that close to them."

Sarah shook her head back and forth, "Maybe you're not, but I am. We have been living together forever now and I really like him. I love him. This is what I want."

John sat there silently for a few minutes absorbing everything that this implied. His mind wandered to their parents and what they would want him to think and feel, and how they would expect him to act. He fully knew his parents would like Anthony. He was well mannered, extremely responsible and above all else loyal. That was what every brother wanted in the man who would marry their sister. So why was he so hesitant?

"Come on John, what's got you so strung up?" Sarah moved to sit right beside him, her hand on top of his. She held onto him trying to provide comfort and love to his worried heart.

"There is just something. I feel like he is hiding something from you, I just can't support a marriage where it is based on lies."

Sarah laughed, "What could he be lying about? Since he moved in, especially after Sam and Amelia married, we have spent so much time together and talked about everything. There is no way he has any secrets from me."

"You weren't at the meeting today, you didn't see how he and Sam were huddled in a corner talking. I know something is going on, there is something big that he is hiding."

"Did it ever occur to you that maybe they were talking about something personal and they didn't want anyone else to overhear it? Maybe Amelia is pregnant already." Sarah chuckled at her comment knowing that would send Anthony off the deep end if it was actually true.

"You weren't there you didn't see it, I'm telling you something is going on. They are hiding something big Sarah and until I feel like everything is out in the open, I won't allow you to get married."

"If I get Anthony to tell you whatever it is that is bothering him, or that is being kept from you, will that ease your worry and then you can give me away?"

John looked at his sister and smiled, "Yeah sis I suppose if that fear of mine can be put to rest then yeah, I will give you away." The look on her face when she smiled melted his heart, he couldn't tell her no. He leaned over and kissed her on the cheek, "I love you Sarah and I just want to protect you."

"I know that John, I promise everything will be okay."

As if his beckoning was on queue Anthony walked through the front door and saw the two of them sitting on the couch. John instantly changed his demeanor. He was very protective, and it didn't matter that Anthony had been living in this house, he still felt claim over the house and the woman sitting next to him.

"Hey John, everything okay, you look pissed?" Anthony walked over and kissed Sarah before sitting down in the chair across the room from the two siblings.

"Sweetie, John and I were talking about what you and I spoke about today, about the marriage."

"Oh well that explains it," Anthony said, "There is nothing worse than hearing your sister is getting married especially to one of your friends. It's a double whammy am I right man?" Anthony was smiling now and seemed playful, but John's facial expression didn't change. "John?"

"I know you're up to something Anthony. Until I know what that is I won't give my blessing or give my sister to you. In fact, until I know what that is you can't stay here."

"John!" Sarah yelled, "That isn't what we talked about at all."

"Whoa there John," Anthony motioned his two hands in the symbol to whoa that you would give to a horse. "You don't have to go and be so drastic. What made you think I was keeping something from Sarah?"

"Are you?" John insisted.

"I mean everyone has secrets but no secrets that affect her in any way at all."

John crossed his arms and glared at Anthony, "So you and Sam huddling in a corner then running out of the room together had nothing to do with a secret that could affect my sister at all? It looked serious and you clearly didn't want to be overheard based on what I was watching."

"Yes, Sam and I have secrets that yes may or may not affect the community as a whole. But as the originating members we are going to have things between us that others don't know about. That's what happens when you lead. Which is why I discussed with Sarah today the idea of new leadership roles. The ones I brought up at the meeting today."

John was shaking his head back and forth, "Nope Anthony I don't buy it. You are completely wrong, and you know it. This may work on my sister, but it isn't going to work on me. What is it, what is going on? You better lay it all on the line right now before I alert everyone that you're up to something."

"Now wait a minute John you can't just come into my home, no our home and make all these demands." Sarah interjected. "I may not like the idea of him hiding something from me, but he hasn't ever lied to me. You can't treat him like you are, it isn't your job to protect me."

"Sarah let me handle this." Anthony said, "And it is his job, I would do it for Amelia, so I completely get it." Anthony stood up from the chair and started pacing around back and forth. The look on his face told John that whatever he was about to say was bad.

"You see how he's acting, I told you he was guilty Sarah. But you didn't want to listen." John had a smug tone to his tenor, and that didn't help the tension in the room.

"You're kind of right but not really. I do have a secret that does affect our community, but it isn't my secret."

Sarah was the first to ask, "What does that even mean?"

"Sweetheart, it simply means, someone has a secret that I know about. And I haven't shared it."

"Well what is it Anthony Davis, you better tell us right now or you won't be marrying Sarah at all." John's arms were crossed, and his body language was shouting to anyone who could see, that he was ready to fight someone.

"It is going to sound crazy. Sam and I actually spoke today about this secret and we made a group decision to share it."

"A group decision whose group?" John asked.

"Anthony, Amelia, Sam and Sunny, the original four." Sarah answered for her lover.

Anthony nodded, "Yes us four. You see, Sunny agreed to let us share her secret. I am all for sharing, Sam isn't. It was actually Amelia's idea to share. She thinks others may have the same secret if we just brought it up."

"Brought what up?" John questioned.

John glared at Anthony non-stop, he wouldn't remove his eyes from his friend. He watched as he moved back to the chair and sat down, ending his pacing.

"Before I tell you, John, you have to promise that you won't mention it at all to anyone. Sunny will tell people with Amelia in their own way and time. Promise me right now. And Sarah, you know most already, there is just some new developments for you."

"Oh man that sounds scary." Sarah coolly said.

"Depends on the secret." John said. No one could fault him for being honest, he wasn't going to play games. If others deserved to know then he would make sure they were told.

With a sigh Anthony started talking. "Just let me talk, let me finish. Ask your questions at the end, because I am afraid if you ask I will get derailed. Can you at least agree to that John?"

He agreed, "Yep, that I can promise you."

Anthony ran his hands through his hair and shook his head back and forth. "Sunny is a witch. I know it seems crazy, it took us a minute or two to get used to the idea and believe it. But we have actually seen her at work and we know she has certain powers. They are growing more powerful each day."

Sarah started to say something, but Anthony raised his hand up, "No wait." He stood from the chair and started pacing again, "You see, she noticed it back before we were a community. She could control the weather. At first it was just coincidences, when she was sad it would rain. But then it got more intense. She can definitely control elements. I thought kids across the street would realize it when their house caught on fire and she was controlling the fire. She has also ensured we always have enough water in our little community, and when that hurricane hit. Well, the hurricane was natural causes, but it may have been intensified by Sunny."

When Sarah started to speak again Anthony raised his hand again signaling her to wait so he could continue. "Her powers are adapting and now she is having these dreams. The reason I want to get guns is because she is now having I guess it's called a premonition of an invasion. There are two men leading the way, a father, Laken and his son, Collins. She knows their names from her dreams. She can also astro-project and she has been going to the library with Amelia to look up all this stuff. It's genetic and I am not totally sure on how that works, Amelia could explain that one to you. There that's it. Now you can ask questions."

Sarah and John sat there in silence. Anthony had moved back to his chair and John thought he could see relief in his friends face after getting all of that out.

"So, we need to prepare for an invasion that's what you're saying?" John asked.

"Yep, John that's exactly what I am saying."

"Does she know when we are going to be attacked?"

Anthony motioned with his shoulders a maybe, "John, it isn't an exact thing, she gets these dreams. What she knows for certain is these two men will be here in maybe two months, and we better be ready for them. Oh, and these men, they are adults. They also have other adults with them."

Both John and Sarah looked up at him square in his eyes and said, "Adults?"

Anthony moved his head up and down, "Yep, and she says the one named Collins is the reason everyone is dead."

John chewed on all of this new information for a minute letting it soak in. Part of him was proud that he knew there was something amiss and someone was lying. The other part of him wished he had never of asked. Because what was he going to do with that information now? He had no idea. All he could do was throw his hat in the ring and help Anthony and Sam defend their home anyway they could.

"Alright Anthony, tell me what you need me to do."

Sarah smiled, and Anthony said, "John, I need you to help Sam and me with fortifying the neighborhood, and I have no idea yet on how we are going to do that."

With a simple nod John had thrown his hat into Anthony's ring and that was that.

It was a simple clearing of the throat that made both guys look at Sarah, "So does that mean I am now officially betrothed?"

"Yeah, I guess it does sis."

Chapter Fourteen -
The Witch Hunt

THE TASK OF SEEKING out others with magical powers wasn't easy. Amelia had realized the chore would be daunting, but she hadn't realized exactly what it would require of Sunny. At first it was easy, they had started with John since Anthony had told him what happened last Thursday. John didn't act shocked or that Sunny was crazy. He asked her a lot of questions about how her dreams felt and what Astro-projection actually was. Sunny enjoyed speaking to him about it because of his curiosity.

It was when they went to Natalie's clan that there were some issues. Her friend Jody seemed skeptical. It didn't matter how many questions she asked, it always ended with her saying science would never uphold what Sunny was claiming. Which was exactly what Sunny was trying to show, that science can't explain what was happening.

Everything took a drastic turn into the weird, when Natalie's brother Brody, came into the conversation. It was Sunny who shocked everyone when she said, "It's time to tell them Brody."

Natalie's face immediately went firm and worried, Jody looked confused and Amelia didn't know what to think. "What do you mean tell them?" Amelia asked.

"I mean, Brody is like me." Sunny stated

"No, he isn't," Natalie said sounding defensive.

"Yes, he is." Sunny stood firm with her hands balled into fists and her arms handing down her sides. Amelia couldn't decide if she was in more of a fight or flight mood. She was hoping the former of the two.

"I can talk for myself, Natalie." Brody said in a calm voice.

Everyone turned to look at him and it was almost as if everyone was holding their breath until his next words were out. "So, tell her." Sunny encouraged.

"Brody, what is she talking about?" Natalie's tone changed to that of the concerned sister instead of the pissed off chaperone.

All he did was shrug, "I don't know what all I can do, I just know that when Sunny makes it rain I can block it, so the rain doesn't fall on me."

"He shields," Sunny offered up. "I think he can shield from magic, but I haven't really tested it much."

Natalie was the first to jump on this prompt, "Have you really tested it at all?"

"Just the rain thing, it's like he's walking around with an invisible umbrella," Sunny smiled, "except when the rain isn't because of me. That's funny because he always gets soaking wet when it's that case. One day he was soaked head to toe and just didn't believe it wasn't me."

Brody stuck his tongue out at Sunny then questioned, "I still think you tricked me!"

Amelia looked between the two kids, back and forth, and finally asked, "Sunny why didn't you tell me?"

"It wasn't my secret, just like this wasn't anyone else's to tell about me."

Natalie walked over to her brother and picked him up and held onto him.

"Ew let me go, Nat, let me go!" Brody wiggled in her arms.

"Quiet you I need to hold you right now."

Jody started to shake her head, "I don't believe it, and I want to see it." She let her comment come out flatly.

"Okay" Sunny and Brody both responded simultaneously to the request.

"We can do it in the back yard, your garden needs water. Come on let's go outside." Sunny said as she and Brody ran through the house to the back yard.

"Amelia, this is crazy." Natalie said as the adults walked through the house.

"Crazy isn't the word Natalie, it is a hoax." Jody declared.

"Wait until you see what they have to do before you cast judgements. If you really are concerned, then have them do some of the experiments on you too." Amelia stated.

"Okay I will."

The three ladies made it out to the back yard and the two kids were all ready and waiting for their audience. "Come on Brody let's show them." Sunny said.

"Wait a second, I'm doing it too. Show me that you can do this by letting me be a part of the experiment." Jody told them.

Sunny lined up both Brody and Jody in a line, about one foot apart. She thought really hard and the cloud began to form over both of their heads. It was two separate clouds that started as one large one. When the rain started there were light sprinkles that hit both Brody and Jody. After about three or four seconds Brody's rain drops suddenly stopped hitting him. It appeared as if they were deflected away from him and rolled off an invisible shield and onto the ground.

Jody on the other hand was getting wet. Her shirt was now stuck against her body and her jeans were soaked. "I think the point is proven" Natalie said laughing at the image in front of her.

"Not quite, hold on." Sunny said. She walked over and looked at Brody then smiled, "Stop Jody's rain from hitting her too."

A couple seconds later Body's shield had left him and now Jody was having her rain deflected off of her. She looked up at the single cloud in aghast shock. "Wow" she said.

"Brody you're getting soaked now!" Natalie hollered out.

"Oh, my bad!" He said and then suddenly both of them had their invisible shields over their heads deflecting the rain.

"So, what do you think now?" Amelia asked the other two ladies standing there in shock. "Is it all a joke or do these two have some powers we may need to harness?"

Jody stormed off from under the rain cloud and said on her way into the house "I still think its crap, but I need to change."

Amelia and Sunny laughed as they watched Jody walk off. While she was away Sunny took this moment to explain to Natalie, in great detail, about the dreams and the feelings she had been getting after each one. Brody said that while he hadn't had any dreams, he was experiencing weird sensations that didn't make any sense to him. Sunny and Amelia felt like it had to be the same thing that had been bothering Sunny. Something was on their way to their small little community and they were going to have to defend it.

"Well count me in, whatever you all need." Natalie had said as the four of them walked into the house.

"Me too!" Hollered Brody.

Amelia smiled at the two of them, siblings were so special especially now. "I'm glad we told you. Now there are no more secrets. Telling the rest will be hard since I am not close to them, and neither is Sunny."

"We aren't close." Natalie pointed out.

"No, but Sunny and Brody are and that made it easier."

Jody came down the stairs in a fresh pair of clothing and her hair brushed backwards in a ponytail. "What did I miss?"

"Just news of our world here being invaded by two jerk men, so nothing new." Natalie laughed. "Can I get you a beer?" She asked Amelia.

"Beer? What?" Amelia's shocked face made Natalie and Jody laugh.

"Yeah, you heard of the stuff?"

"Yeah. I just, didn't think anyone drank it. I mean, it isn't exactly legal." Amelia blushed out of embarrassment.

"What do you think will happen? The cops from the past will come and arrest us for being dubious?"

"No, I mean, maybe, hell I don't know. Okay fine give me one."

Sunny's face perked up when Amelia said yes. She looked over at her pseudo sister and gave an inquisitive look.

"Don't tell Sam." Amelia instructed as she opened the can of Miller Lite and took a sip. "Wow, okay yuck."

Natalie and Jody both laughed at her and somehow this light bit of fun made everything okay.

"Maybe we should head home. I will tell Sam that you're down to help. I am sure he and Anthony have plans in the work. I know John was willing to help as well. Thanks for not making fun of Sunny."

"Look Amelia I know we aren't close, but I wouldn't pick on a kid. The kids are who need us most of all. And if this is all true, sounds like we will need each other. Maybe you and I should get to know each other better." Natalie stopped talking to look at the two kids in the room. "Especially if those two are going to be together."

"How do you know that?" Amelia asked.

"Call it a hunch. I'll see you all around." She winked at Amelia and then walked her to the front door. "See you next time Sunny."

After Amelia and Sunny left Brody looked up at his sister, "You lied."

"I did not, I just didn't tell." Natalie said with pride in her tone.

"Why not, you can see they just want help. You can trust them."

"Not yet I can't kid. Remember we are always going to put our family first so until I can ensure that Anthony and company have the same interest as ours then we will keep this unique tool chested, okay?"

Brody walked off mad at his sister, "This isn't right they came here looking for help and all you did was let Jody find out about me."

Jody was still in the room and now looking at her friend in a puzzled expression. "I feel like I am missing something Natalie."

"Because you are. She's a witch too." Brody said and stormed off.

"You're what? No way! How have I known you forever and I never knew that?"

Natalie shrugged her shoulders, "Just because I am not talking about it with people like Brody and Sunny do doesn't mean anything. I just don't want everyone making a big deal out of it."

"What can you do?" Jody's sudden skepticism had seemed to vanish, and she was now engrossed in her friends abilities.

"I can see the future, not like Sunny in dreams but when I touch people or objects." Natalie shrugged her shoulders, "It's really no big deal, and it doesn't happen a lot."

"You sound like that show Charmed that used to be on television." Jody started looking at her friend oddly.

"See that look right there that's why I never told you, I didn't want any looks!"

Jody argued, "I'm not giving you a look!"

"Yes, you are, I can feel it all about you, it's grazing all over my aura and I don't like it! Stop it now!"

Jody rolled her eyes, "I'm going to tell you like Sunny told Brody, you gotta tell them."

"Eventually but just not yet, I'm keeping this secret close to the chest so that means you can't tell either."

Jody lifted her right hand up into the air and held up three fingers, "Scouts honor" and then walked out of the room.

Natalie didn't like that her secret was now getting out. She had kept it to herself for so long and then only to Brody, that's how she wanted it to stay. But the moment she had shook John's hand the day they met, she knew it would eventually change and her secret would be out. The image she got in her head the moment they touched would haunt her forever. She saw Brody laying in her arms, blood dripping down his forehead, she could feel the agony inside of her. She wasn't sure at the time what that image meant. She almost didn't follow John and Anthony to this compound, but she had known in her bones that was meant to happen.

One day her and John would fulfill the other premonition that she had about him, but she wasn't ready to face that either. She wasn't looking for romance, she didn't want any partners or any complications. Her life was good the way it was, and she didn't like change.

But she knew change would happen soon enough, she hadn't yet found a way to postpone it. But what she really needed to do, was change the future. She hoped that by not being with John what she saw about Brody would change as well.

If she never took a lover, she would always be there to protect her brother.

"SAM, ANTHONY, YOU TWO in here?" Amelia called out as her and Sunny walked into their home.

"Yep we are in the storage room." Sam yelled.

"How did it go" Anthony asked as he walked into the hall-way to greet his sister and pseudo sister Sunny.

With a shrug Amelia observed, "I mean, it went well."

"Not that last part, that was weird." Sunny looked up at Amelia, "I know you know what I mean."

Amelia nodded her head, "Yeah Natalie is def up to some-thing. It was strange. But Brody! Brody can shield it was super cool."

Sam opened his arms as he walked into the hallway to join all of them and Amelia walked right into them. She gave him a soft kiss on his lips and he caressed the small of her back. "Hey you," he whispered just for her to hear. "I missed you."

Amelia let her smile widen and she gave him a longer kiss this time and whispered back, "I missed you more."

"Excuse me love birds, but we have official business to dis-cuss." Anthony said.

"You will have to ignore them, they are like this all the time." Sunny rolled her eyes as she made the obvious statement.

"I think I know what's going on with Natalie," Amelia looked proud of herself. "I think she is a witch too. I don't know how to prove it, but she seemed very sure that Sunny and Brody were going to end up involved with one another. She al-so seemed like she was faking shock and surprise when we told her about Sunny. She was way to understanding."

"Was anyone else there?" Anthony asked.

"Jody was, and she didn't believe me at all." Sunny supplied.

"Exactly Jody was totally skeptical and wanted hard core proof. Natalie on the other had was all chill about it. I'm telling you, she is a witch too. It's like a witch hunt, who can find the most first."

Sam scrunched his face up at his wife's last comment, "I don't know if I would put it like that, it sounds like kinda Salemish if you say it like that. Not a good thing. We're not gonna hunt them down and kill them."

"You know what I mean Sam. I'm telling you something is amiss over there and I am going to find out what it is."

Anthony shook his head, "Sam you better control your woman because we have more important things to do than monitor her little bag of crazy ideas."

"Hey, she was your sister, you can control her too." Sam retorted.

"She's still my sister, but you claimed her that day you said, 'I Do.'"

"Guys I am kinda standing right here, and I can control myself." Amelia said.

Sunny was the first to laugh and then they all let out a few chuckles. "I'll be good I promise." Amelia said.

"Just so long as we prepare for whatever is coming up. Sunny's dream seems very real and now that we know we have two, maybe three witches at least in the community it makes me really believe her dreams." Sam said.

Anthony piggybacked on Sam's comments by saying, "Today was really successful with John. The three of us went out and collected our first round of ammunition and guns. Hopefully over the week we will be able to acquire more. We're going to make this place a fortress."

"Let me guess, like *The Walking Dead*." Sunny rolled her eyes as she said it.

"Exactly, but better because we saw where they went wrong." Sam said proudly.

"Oh boy, this is going to be a long week." Amelia teased.

"It will be, so we will all need sleep and food. We can hold off telling anyone else for a day so you two can work on food supplies for our two families and then the store. Oh yeah, I need underwear, sis can you get me some please?"

"Anthony, I believe you have a little woman at home to do those tasks." Amelia teased her brother.

"I do, but she told me to do it so now I am asking you."

Amelia rolled her eyes and waved her hand off at her brother, "You're so lazy, and sure I will get you your boxers for the month. Now I am going to go take a bath, no one mess with the water supply I am sticky and need to relax."

After her departure from the family she walked up the stairs alone and had a feeling in her stomach, something was going to happen, and soon.

Chapter Fifteen-
You're Never Too
Prepared

JOHN AND SAM HAD SPENT the last couple days walking around their small part of Florida looking for guns. Thankfully they had found an Academy that had a decent stock of hand guns and ammunition still intact. They also picked up some crossbows and regular compound bows. They hadn't figured out quite how to make the arrows work in sizing, but they gathered as many as they could to deal with that at a later date.

Up to this point they had acquired one hundred hand guns, twenty-six shot guns and seven rifles. They were in desperate need of target practice though since only a couple people had ever been on a hunt before. They made mandatory shooting practice a daily thing for one hour a day for each person over the age of twelve. They practiced with the bows and the guns.

Sam had been in charge of designing a layout for watchmen and where they were to be stationed, along with some sort of signaling mechanism to make sure that no one caught them off guard. They had picked up some of the hand radios and batteries. Everyone was pleased to discover that they still worked. There were ones with a two-mile radius and a five-mile radius. That's how they determined where to put the look outs.

Over the past year they had accumulated more people than just the handful the group started out with. Of the individuals over twelve they had twenty-one. The usual suspects were the team leaders. Anthony, Sam, John and Natalie each had a team of two other people. That meant twelve people were on look-out duty at any given time. They had eight hour shifts and that was now their job instead of tilling the gardens or going out scouting for supplies.

One older teen, she was sixteen, her name Garcia, stayed out of the rotation. Amelia and Sarah thought it would be important, especially for the young kids, to maintain a school house. They turned one home into a school and Garcia taught classes. Each age group had a different schedule for schooling. Anyone under the age of twelve was expected to attend with no exceptions. Sarah insisted that this would allow for their world to keep on living.

Even if what they were teaching was limited to the current 'elders' knowledge base. There was a lot of making it up as they went along, eventually, once life had settled down, each person on the lookout team would teach a class. As a group they all recognized that certain people could specialize in specific fields. Anthony insisted that they take advantage of this.

Amelia taught crop harvesting and storage. She specialized on the right months to plant crops, how to rotate harvests by location and most important, how to keep it from spoiling throughout the year. Natalie had a session on mechanics. They all learned how to take apart a specific part of a vehicle and put it back together. All the basics that were needed when changing oil and basic skills to maintain their construction equipment.

Jody's class was required by everyone, she conducted basic first aid and CPR. She had been certified by Red Cross only a month before the world took a dive into the apocalypse. She even found a supply store with the dummy bodies for practice.

Sunny wasn't a fan of school, she felt it was beneath her. There was a struggle to get her to participate but eventually peer pressure wore her out. Now she was learning all about fractions and the proper way to formulate sentences.

Each of these classes lasted for two hours a day for an eight week rotation. That way everyone got the opportunity to learn something new and gave the other instructors a break for most of the year when it came to creating lessons.

Amelia and Sarah were in charge of the supplies and they always went out together, never separate. Jody headed up the medical portions of things, that left five other people in charge of the farming. It wasn't ideal but it had to be done like this. They were worried about an attack and this was the only way to ensure everyone was prepared.

Because of how important it was to make sure everyone stayed in communication they had the team leaders rotating on which ones were in charge of the communications while others were out. Each leader would work two eight hour shifts a day with alternating days off with just one shift. It sucked, they all hated it. But you could never be too prepared Anthony kept saying.

Things took a few weeks to get everything settled in with regards to the schedules, but once they had a rhythm, everyone discovered that it almost felt natural. The little community had grown into a well-oiled family. They all had their parts and trust was beginning to really flourish.

The younger kids had their parts too. They were helping to weed the gardens, fold clothing, and stacking supplies. No one went on without contributing something. They were all willing and ready to help.

Amelia and Sunny had made their way through each of the families in their community. Outside of Sunny, Brody and potentially Natalie they had found two other people with magical powers. One nineteen-year-old and one younger child. John had been skeptic at first with all of the talk about magic, after seeing their little army of magical people start to form, it was hard to deny the truth that was staring them right in the face.

"Hey man what's got your mind so wrapped up?" Sam asked John as they were preparing to go out on their next scavenging mission.

"Just thinking about how much has changed in the last two months. We went from an easy community to one that is preparing for battle. Just seems weird."

Sam nodded his head in agreement, "Yeah, but something about what we have now just feels right, like in my gut feels right."

"Sarah had said the same thing the other day. Maybe the structure? You know how people love consistency."

John grinned, "Yeah, you may be onto something there, good point." He was putting together his bag of supplies and looked up at Sam, "You know we need to find the horses or some other form of transportation right?"

Sam smiled, "What the ten speeds aren't working for you anymore?"

That made John laugh, "Yeah, man, but you know how little we can actually do with a bike."

"Amelia laughs every time, she says we need to go build a horse drawn carriage from the eighteen hundreds. Who knew in the year twenty eighteen we would need to go back in time and use basic technology over the modern tech we grew up on?"

"I guess, Sam, that's what makes this the end of the world, we're digressing." John smirked to himself at the joke he made.

"I was looking at a map this morning, one I found at one of the gas stations. There is a patch of land that didn't have any roads along it. I don't think it has buildings either. I wanted to check it out and see if maybe we could be lucky and find livestock." Sam zipped his supply bag up and hoisted it on his shoulder.

"Sure, whatever you want to try I'm game for." John followed suit hoisting his bag onto his back. "Just so long as I am home for dinner. Sarah and Anthony are having me over and I want to give him hell, you know the big brother stuff before they get married."

Sam let out a small laugh, "Man go easy on him, that stuff is the worst. I remember how he raked me through the coals and I've grown up with him! It's torture. One day you will see how it is."

"I don't see how I'm not even interested in anyone right now. Not like I have a lot of options either." John walked over to look at his bicycle, he started to check the tires for air.

"What about Natalie?"

"What about her?" John looked in the opposite direction of Sam.

"You seem to be avoiding the topic here John."

"So, let's get going. No need to gossip."

Sam's right eyebrow quirked upward questioning his friend, "Whatever you say man, but I think there is clearly a story to tell."

"Nope no story. Come on." Sam began walking towards the gate while pushing his bicycle, "We do really need to find another form of transportation."

"That's the goal man, come on."

The two of them rode out of the safety of their compound on their bicycles heading west. Sam lead the way hoping that the bit of land he found would actually work for them. He had estimated that the land was about ten miles out of town and they were five miles from the town border. About an hour and a half after they left the compound the two of them found the plot that Sam had identified.

It was more than they could have hoped for, it was an abandoned dairy farm. There were cows, calves and horses roaming around in the pasture. There were chickens from the sounds they were hearing, and Sam knew in his gut he would find more once they started to explore.

"I can't believe you actually found something." John said as he set his bicycle up against one of the wooden posts outside of the barn.

"No kidding I mean what were the odds?" Sam was looking around the farm trying to take in what all he saw.

"Look there are four horses, four Sam. Can you imagine what we could do with that!"

Sam was smiling ear to ear, all he could think about was how Amelia would tease him about building the wagon next. "Yeah we really can do something with this. Let's hope we can figure out how to saddle them and get them back home."

"Hey maybe they have the buggy your wife is talking about." John teased.

"God could I be so lucky!" Sam joked.

The two of them spent the next hour going through the farm looking through the barn supplies for the livestock. It was obvious no one had been tending to things since the feed was still well stocked and unused. The previous owners did have a buggy of sorts, but it wasn't the kind that Amelia kept teasing about. But it would do; and he was fairly certain that the girls would be able to turn it into the kind of buggy from the game Oregon Trail.

"Where are we going to keep all of these animals?" John asked.

"I think we could house them in the south west part of our neighborhood, you know opposite where the gardens are."

"It isn't like our neighborhood is equipped honestly to have livestock. We have the land size just, a lot of concrete. These animals are going to need grass." John was looking through all of the supplies and counting out different sections of stuff.

"Let's take the horses. If the scouts each rode a horse then they could graze out on their trails and rides which would cut back on the need for them to do it at home, yeah?"

"Okay Sam that isn't a bad idea. What about the cows?"

They looked at each other for a few minutes while John watched Sam process through his thoughts.

"I think the key is going to be how many cows are we going to take back with us?"

"I think we need at least what three?" John said.

"So, go with me on this, what if we take three neighboring houses and remove the fencing from the inside parts of the back yard and give them that grass to roam on. At least for now."

John nodded his head a few times and then pointed to the stall behind Sam. "And what about that big guy?"

Sam turned around and shrugged, "I don't know about the bull yet. We can't take him with us today so maybe we could give that project to Anthony to work on. We can radio back home when we are five miles out and tell them what we're bringing. Give them a chance maybe to work on removing those fences."

"Well this is a good start. And what about the chickens, I'm thinking we could fence in one of the front yards and build a coop with the wood from the back yards." John had started walking towards the coop. "And in the meantime," John picked up a basket sitting around and started filling it with eggs. "We're having scrambled eggs for breakfast at my house tomorrow," he was grinning ear to ear at the thought of something new to eat that wasn't fruit.

"I think bringing the four horses and three cows back today with us along with the supplies we loaded up is enough. We can come back tomorrow for more."

"We will probably need to take it easy with the horses at first since they have clearly not been used in the last year." John said.

"Good point. However, it will still be faster to get home with the horses pulling the buggy than by bicycle."

"Amen to that brother, let's load up and get home." John finally felt something changing, he wasn't feeling like it was all doom and gloom. "Hey, we should look in the house for first aid supplies while we are here. Just in case someone else shows up. I know Jody could use anything extra."

"Good call, a working farm I am sure had some good stuff especially for the animals."

Once the two were finished loading up the buggy with the feed and other supplies they hoisted their bikes onto the platform and tied everything down securing their load. Getting the horses to cooperate enough to attach to the buggy was harder to do. The buggy only had room for two horses up front. Sam had decided that he could ride one of the horses with the saddle so that left the fourth free.

"We can tie it to the back of the buggy like they used to do in those western movies." John suggested.

Shrugging Sam said, "Sure, but make sure you don't ride them all too hard pulling the heavy buggy."

"I know, I know sheesh." John found the bench where he had to sit uncomfortable. "If I am going to do this a lot I'll need a cushion for this thing."

"You don't think they have one in the shed somewhere?"

"No idea, I didn't look." John hopped off the buggy, "Give me five."

Sam waited patiently for his friend to return. As he was waiting he saw a dog walking around one side of the farm. He dismounted from the horse and walked over towards the dog. It wasn't really a puppy, it looked full grown, full grown and scared.

"Hey there boy, come here, I won't hurt you." He said in a calmed tone voice. He reached his hand out for the dog to sniff him. The fur was golden, and that made Sam think he must be a golden retriever. "You want to come home with me, I have a little girl that would love to meet you."

The dog walked slowly towards Sam and eventually accepted his hand by sniffing and then licking it. "Good boy, good boy." He let Sam pat the top of his head lightly. "Come on, let's get you home." Sam turned around to walk back to the horses and slapped his leg a couple times and called out, "Come boy."

The dog ambled his way along with Sam and then suddenly without warning jumped into the front of the buggy where John was sitting.

"What's this?" He asked.

"Sunny, she needs a friend and I think this guy here needs one too." Sam started to mount the horse again, "She will love it."

John was looking the dog over and petting it slowly, "Well I am sure Sunny will love it but it's a girl and she is pregnant."

Sam shot his head back, "How in the world could you possibly know that?"

"Well genius first I looked between the legs and didn't see any parts that only men have. And second, I put my hand on her stomach and felt little paws kicking."

"I guess then all the kids will be getting a new puppy for Christmas." Sam rolled his eyes, "Lucky us. Now come on let's get home."

"Wait, the cows!" John hollered out.

"Crap, we forgot to get them set up." Sam shook his head back and forth and dismounted from the horse. "How are we going to get them home?"

"What if we took one of those trailers that you carry horses in and just hooked the horses up to that?"

"I have no idea if that will work, I mean, I guess it would." Sam ran his hand through his hair and walked over to the vehicle storage facility and called out to John. "I have an even better idea, look what I found." He pushed open the door all the way to display a truck already attached to one of the trailers John was talking about.

"Damn I'm good." John laughed, "See I told you that would be a great idea. We can load part of the coup and chickens up in the bed of that truck too. How's the gas?"

Sam opened the front door and looked inside, he found the keys stuck in the visor, turning the key switch into he on position he belted out, "Hey it's even full!"

"Wow we can make several trips then! Hell yeah!"

Sam walked around the truck and inspected the tires and then the connection to the trailer. "Let's load these cows up and get home. We're gonna be heroes!"

Anthony was the one who caught the radio call from Sam and John about their discovery. He quickly went into action with the fencing. He, Natalie and Jody were the only ones around that were available to help tear down the fencing. They each took a section, he hadn't expected it to be as tedious and physically demanding as it turned out to be. Anthony and Natalie had their sections completed by the time that they showed up. Natalie went to help Jody finish her part.

It had seemed too good to be true to Anthony, their community now had actual livestock. Amelia would make a run to the library to acquire all the books on milking cows and making cheese. He could see her enjoying learning all of that. They were going to need more horses that he already knew for sure. He and Sam would figure out the best way to distribute using the horses.

"Hey guys, great find!" Anthony said as his friends pulled into the neighborhood. "Oh, Amelia is going to just love that buggy!"

"I know I can already hear her teasing me in my head over it."

It took all four of them to get the cows to go into the back yards but once they were in there they seemed to be okay. Jody had found a wheel barrel in one of the garages, they used that to pour feed into for them. Who knew if they were just hungry or starving but Anthony seemed confident they needed the feed immediately. If nothing he said it would help them feel safe.

"Did you figure out what we are going to do with the horses yet?" John asked Anthony.

"No, but I figure maybe we can tie them up to something over in the play area and we just keep the kids away for today. We can build something I'm sure if we all work at it."

Sam and John nodded in agreement. As they continued to unload they were interrupted with a scream of laughter. All of them knew who had just gotten home, the girls.

"Sam, you got me a buggy!" Amelia screamed out as she came walking over to them.

"Oh boy, you're in for the teasing now buddy." John mumbled under his breath. Sam punched him in the shoulder as he walked past his friend to greet his wife.

"I sure did and that isn't all brought home." He turned around towards the buggy and yelled, "Come here girl!"

The dog peeked his head up and when Sam clapped his hands she jumped out of the buggy and ran towards him. "Where's Sunny?"

"She's in the house she will be right out, she had to go to the bathroom. You got her a dog, that's so sweet."

"Correction, I got her a pregnant dog, so lots of kids will be getting puppies." Sam grinned and let out a laugh.

"Oh boy, well looks like we're gonna be parents then." Amelia smiled. "Sunny will love this."

"I thought she could use someone to offer unconditional love to her without question." Sam reached for her hand and caressed his fingers against hers when they made contact.

"It was a great idea. Here she comes." Amelia waived Sunny over to meet them.

"Hey kiddo, have fun shopping?" Sam asked as he knelt down to get to eye level with his cousin.

"It was okay got a couple things I needed. You got horses, that's awesome Sam."

"I got more than that, here, meet your new friend." When Sam pointed to the dog Sunny's mouth dropped open.

"Really Sam, for me?"

"Yep Sunny, all yours. She's a female and she is pregnant so you're gonna have to help be a momma. What do you think?"

"Wow! I think it's awesome this is the best birthday present ever!"

"What did you say" Amelia interjected.

"It's my birthday, didn't you guys know?"

By this point Jody, Natalie, John, and Anthony had gathered close enough to hear the interchange and they all were looking at one another clearly not knowing what to say.

"Sunny, I ..." Sam got choked up and couldn't speak.

"I'm just teasing Sam it isn't my birthday, but you should have seen your face." Sunny burst into laughter and hugged her cousin. "Really Sam this dog is great, I'm so happy, thank you."

All of the older teens looked at one another and slowly they all started laughing. "You all should have seen all your faces that was great." Sunny laughed some more and then started to run off. "Come on girl come with me and I'll give you a bath."

Once Sunny had left Anthony was the first to speak up. "What's sad is we have no way to confirm what day it actually is. Hell, it could be her birthday."

"One crisis at a time man, let's find a place for the horses then we can work on a calendar." Jody said.

The group of them worked together for the remainder of the day getting a make shift stable set up along with distributing the dozens of eggs that were claimed from the farm. Everyone's excitement increased when they discovered that one of the houses on that back row next to where the cows were being kept had a pool in the back yard that was only three feet deep in most areas. They all agreed they would work on piping in plumbing to that house so they could use it as a watering hole for all of the animals. After much debate they removed all the interior boards from the back yards and placed the three cows and four horses back there. Each block had eight houses so with that much room they were hopeful that the animals would be able to live harmoniously together.

By the end of the day Sam was truly exhausted. He and Amelia walked back to their house hand in hand smiling. The amount of work they managed to get done in such a short time was nothing less than a miracle. But their community had captured a real win with this find.

"You know what we have to do tomorrow right?" Sam said as he took his shoes and socks off.

"Learn to milk the cows?"

He shook his head, "Nope, figure out how to transport the bull."

Amelia laughed and took the remainder of her clothes off, she walked into their bathroom and turned the shower on. "You got that job all to yourself now. I want no part of that."

When Sam moved to sit on the bed Amelia yelled out, "Don't you dare sit on my bed Sam! You're a right mess."

He rolled his eyes at her, "Woman, I brought you a horse and buggy just like you asked for, now let me just sleep."

Chapter Sixteen- How Life Settles and Changes

NOT EVERYONE WAS OKAY with the newest additions to the neighborhood. Natalie's back yard seemed prime for the chickens to continuously break into and hid out. She was constantly having to call on John to get him to come and rescue them. It was during the third rescue that she realized this was how they ended up getting together, today of all days. She had touched his shoulder and saw it, saw them kissing next to the chicken coup. She was still trying with all of her might to keep anything from happening, but she wasn't having much luck.

She was still scared to death for Brody, but she had been doing a lot of soul searching. Her other fear was she fought so hard against allowing her and John to develop that she wondered if that could be the cause for the future she saw for her brother. She didn't know how to reconcile all the driving parts so she had decided to simply give up. She would let the fates dictate what happened.

Or at least she tried to...

"Hey there, we gotta stop meeting like this." John said to her as he walked into her back yard with a pile of wood planks hoisted on his shoulders.

She gave a nonchalant shrug, "Maybe I keep sabotaging the panels to let the chickens in as an excuse to call you." Natalie smiled at him as she teased.

"You know, all you have to do, if that's what you want, is just ask me out on a date. I'm not old fashioned I'll gladly let the women lead." He set the wood down from his shoulders next to the side of the house.

"I'm just teasing, I hate these darn chickens. Get rid of them please!"

"Awe man, and here I thought we were making some headway, you know, you and me."

Natalie tilted her head to the left and quirked her eyebrows up, "What do you mean you and me?"

"Ya know, you" John pointed at her then aimed his finger at himself, "and me. An item."

"I'm not sure what you're talking about." She tried to play coy.

"Don't you do that, you know exactly what I mean, you and me, we have chemistry." John pulled his hammer out of the tool belt he was wearing and pointed it in the position against the plank already up against the fence and started removing the nail. He worked at it until the whole plank was on the ground and he had a pile of nails started in his pocket.

"I think you're mistaken John, I need you for chicken removal only." Natalie's heart started to speed up, she really wasn't ready for this, ready for what was going to follow. She had dreamed about it and she had known it would happen but knowing and living the experience were two different things.

John didn't say anything else, he simply worked on the fence rebuild section by section. He had offered to replace the fence for her in his down time. Which today he managed to have three hours he could devote to her. He had traded with Anthony three hours of his supervisory shift for tomorrow, so he could get this job done. He was exhausted, but this would be well worth it for him.

"You hungry John?" Natalie had asked almost an hour into his work. He had managed to replace a third of the panels and the job looked really well done.

"Yeah, actually, I am."

"Why don't you stop and come eat with me. I made some dinner and I thought it would be a nice thank you."

John didn't have to be asked twice, he dropped his hammer down on the pile of planks and walked over to where Natalie was standing. "Mighty nice of you, can I wash up in your bathroom?"

"Of course, why don't you use mine, Brody and the other kids like to keep theirs messy and Jody has the other guest bathroom. Wouldn't want to impose on them."

John let his lips form a sly smile, he felt like this was a small victory, getting to use her personal bathroom instead of the guest one. "Thank you, ma'am, mighty kind of you."

Natalie rolled her eyes and walked into the house, wiggling her finger for John to follow. When she opened the master bedroom that was stationed downstairs she guided him into the bathroom area. She opened a cabinet and pulled out a large towel. "If you want to shower, you can. I haven't used my allotment of water yet today."

"My hands will be sufficient, I tend to take long showers, and maybe you could join me sometime." He winked at her and then walked over to the sink. He squirted some soap into his hands and rubbed them together lathering them up. With his pinky he switched on the faucet and the cold water hit his skin as he cleaned the soap suds off his hands.

Natalie noticed he didn't avert his gaze from his task at hand. She was smiling at him, but he wouldn't notice it. This was getting easier and easier the flirting and that unsettled her. "I'll be in the kitchen when you're ready to eat."

As she walked through her bedroom she took a look around, she was proud of the well-kept house she managed. Everything had a place and that's where it was stored. She sometimes wondered if her bedroom even looked lived in since it was never untidy. She stepped back into the kitchen and the smell of dinner hit her, it was lingering the air.

She had pulled out two plates and set them down at the table along with two wine glasses she liked to use for tea. When he walked into the kitchen she looked up and smiled, this time he noticed. His return smile made her heart jump a beat and that caused her stomach to feel flutters. Crap, she wasn't ready for this.

"That smells fantastic, do I detect some type of stew?" John asked as he sat down across from her at the table.

Natalie smiled, "Yes, it's my own little concoction that I'm quite proud of."

"It smells like heaven, what's in it?" John held his bowl up patiently waiting for her to take the spoon and scoop some into his dish.

"Well I have the fresh veggies from the garden in here along with some spices that I have been growing on my own. I also found the jack pot one day and landed on some beef stew soup at the grocery store. I've kept it for quite a while for a special occasion. Guess getting a new fence is that occasion."

"Thank you, Natalie. I am touched you would spend your precious stew on me."

She felt her cheeks blush, "It's not a problem really, and you're doing all that work for me."

"It's truly my pleasure. Anything for you."

The two of them ate in silence, John didn't know what to say to fill the void. He was nervous as can be waiting for the next moves to happen. He had no idea how to do this. He had teased and joked about it with the guys but now that he was face to face with destiny he didn't want to screw it up.

As far as soups go, this one wasn't bad. The beef stew tasted great, he couldn't remember how long it had been since he had that. Sam said they had soup all the time, but his woman was one of the ones in charge of scavenging supplies, so they always had the best stuff. John didn't care about that stuff, he was single. But if this was how people who were paired off together ate then maybe he had been the dumb one for putting this off so long.

He could really get used to life like this. Coming home from a long hard day's work to a woman who smelled like her, and cooked like this. A home that was warm and welcoming. This was what dreams were made of and he was really starting to fall hard for this woman.

All she was really missing was a real private garden, she had the herbs but she needed more vegetables. Ones that went fast in the common area so that meant there wasn't lots to go around. Or maybe she could have wheat fields, she could make flour, he bet she was great with bread products.

"John, are you even listening to me?"

The sound of Natalie's voice snapped John back into the moment. He had drifted off on his imaginary life with Natalie and their own little farm he hadn't heard anything that she said.

"I'm sorry, I was daydreaming. Blame your stew it is that good." He tried to smile, but he had felt bad that he had completely ignored her like that.

Luckily Natalie chuckled and smiled, "Well then I shall take it as a complement. What I had said was, do you like cobbler?"

"Cobbler?" John let his mouth form a grin, "Who doesn't like that?"

"Just checking, I also managed to find some ice cream that the space astronauts use. They had them on a sale display on one of the end caps, some NASA store. Cobbler and ice cream, for my hard-working handy man."

John set his silverware down and looked straight at Natalie, his expression was obviously very serious. "Marry me, Natalie. Right now."

She curled her lips up and let out a healthy hearty laugh, "What?"

"You made me cobbler, with ice cream I cannot let a woman like you go." He reached his hand out and gestured for her to put her hand with his. When she complied he continued, "I mean it, you're amazing. And maybe not married right this moment, but, let me court you."

"Did you just say court?" That made her laugh again.

"I did, Sunny told me I needed to work on being a southern gentleman, so I am doing as the mighty kid suggests."

"Well in that case shouldn't you ask my oldest living male relative permission first, if we are doing it all formally?" She was teasing him.

"I already got Brody's blessing, why do you think he's off with Sunny today?"

Natalie was speechless, and the smirk on John's face told her that he knew he had gotten to her. She was a goner and there was nothing anyone could do to change that, she realized.

"Well, I guess I have no other option but to say yes, John, I'll let you court me. But there are rules!"

"There are always rules when it comes to your gender." It was his turn to tease.

"There will be no funny business, I do not have any belief that we will even survive long in this new world and I don't want to be responsible for a baby as well."

John nodded, "Fair enough no sex before marriage." He winked.

Natalie rolled her eyes and then continued, "You won't sleep over here, and I don't want Brody seeing that."

"Fair enough, my bed will always be available, for sleeping." He smirked this time.

"Lastly."

"Oh, there is always a lastly, hit me babe."

She rolled her eyes, "Lastly I expect you to know up front I am always right and disagreeing with me, or calling me babe, is a deadly mistake."

"Why does it seem like you've put thought into this? I only just asked Brody this morning, and he swore he wouldn't tell you."

"Maybe I will tell you my secret, one day, for now, just assume I know everything because I am a woman, hear me roar." She laughed.

"Just give me a chance Natalie, I promise you won't regret it."

She lifted her wine glass that was filled with tea and signaled for him to mimic her. "I just hope you don't change your mind."

As they tapped their glasses together they heard the warning siren that they had installed a couple weeks ago. One blast every fifteen seconds meant that everyone needed to meet at the community center spot for an important announcement.

"What do you think is going on?" Natalie said as she stood up.

"Not sure, but it is just an announcement, so it can't be anyone trying to fight us just yet."

Natalie covered the stew and cleaned off her plate. John brought his to her and offered his assistance. When they were done cleaning, he reached his hand out, "Come on, let's get this kumbaya moment over.

She took his hand without a second thought to it, as they walked through her living room to go out her front door and down the street, until they were at the center of the neighborhood. People were straggling in from all the different houses.

Sam was seated up front and John pulled Natalie in that direction. "Come on, let's get first hand what's going on."

Sam had seen John and Natalie walking up towards him and he nodded in their direction. "Hey guys, what's going on," he asked as he looked that their joined hands.

"Shut up man, you know what's going on." John shook his head and then moved Natalie to sit in the row behind Sam.

"You two aren't always going to be like this are you?" Natalie questioned.

Sam turned around smiling, "Nah, he just gives me crap all the time about Amelia, so I am enjoying this moment of revenge, don't worry Nat it has nothing to do with you." Sam winked at her.

"Don't call me that, it's Natalie."

"Oh, John you certainly got a feisty one, you best be careful." Sam bellowed a laugh at his friend. John took a swing at Sam's arm and Sam had jumped like it hurt, but he was still laughing.

"Idiots." Natalie said under her breath.

John took his seat when he saw Amelia walking up with Sunny in tow. Once everyone had taken their seats, Brody joining Natalie, Anthony walked to the center of the stage and grabbed everyone's attention.

"I always hate being the bearer of bad news, but I have bad news."

The silence in the group was stunning, John knew when people heard this they all held their breath waiting for that shoe to drop.

"As you know Sunny has been the one preparing us, well, last night she had a dream. This time the dream was more specific. She can't explain it, but she knows, the attack will happen in three weeks' time. Three weeks from tomorrow to be exact."

Everyone started talking and looking over at Sunny. John watched Sam put a protective arm around her and Anthony did his best to silence everyone.

"With this new information also came a direction, we know where they are coming from. She saw in her dream a sign from Jacksonville. Now we know where to focus our efforts. Tomorrow there will be a new patrol schedule focusing more on the north this time since we know that's where they are descending from. I hope that each of you are taking seriously our trainings because all of us will have to be on our best game." Anthony paused talking to look around until he found Brody. When he made eye contact he smiled at the kid and then kept talking. "We have someone here who can shield. Sunny believes that Laken and Collins are magical and with that knowledge we know we will need magical assistance to win. Brody has agreed with work with us to shield as many people as he can from magical attacks."

Jody took this moment to raise her hand and ask a question, "You mean like in the movie *Twilight*?"

Anthony nodded, "Yep that's exactly what I mean. So, he is going to spend a little bit of time with everyone. He needs to get to know us all, so he can properly connect with each of us. I know this seems bizarre and out of the norm, but we have to do it." He looked around the audience, "Does anyone else have any other questions, and I know this is a lot to take in but, it's what we have to do."

When no one else answered he nodded at everyone, "Okay then meeting over. Please prepare your homes, check your guns, ammo and supplies. Food included. We have no idea how long this will last. Also, tomorrow we will start re-fortifying the walls for barrier protection. Let's hope that Sunny is wrong and this is all a big misunderstanding."

Everyone slowly left the community spot and John looked over at Natalie, "I think I need to stay and talk with them. This is kinda big and now we will have a lot more to do."

She grinned and squeezed his hand, "Come by tomorrow, I'm making pancakes. Did I mention I have a lot of mixes stored from my scavenging days?"

Her grin was enough to melt his heart, "I'll see you bright and early."

Sam, Anthony and John were all standing together at the front of the speaking area looking around at their community. Sam was the first to break the silence, "No one is taking this from us."

"Agreed" Anthony said.

"But we all know not everyone will make it out of the battle alive. It's almost a given." John hated himself for even making that statement.

"Yeah that's true, but, we have got to do our best. Give it all we have." Anthony's voice started to get shaky as he spoke.

Sam nodded, "What was that saying we learned in U.S. History, 'come and take it' wasn't that it?"

"Pretty sure that is from some rednecks in Texas." John laughed.

"But doesn't it apply, come and take it. That's our battle cry." Anthony said, his voice full of pride.

All together in unison the three of them looked to the front of the gate and repeated the phrase as one.

Come and take it.

Epilogue - How It All Began - August 27, 2017

LAKEN HAD WATCHED THE news all day about the hurricane that was beating down the coast of Texas. The weather was primed for their spells. It wasn't every day that Mother Nature gave the covens the most opportune moment, a chance to tap into the most powerful sources of magic.

At a young age, the lessons of how the world actually worked were instilled on Laken. He was taught the power of three, along with, the power of planet Earth. Everything on this planet is made up of matter he was taught in elementary school. When he came home to his parents to talk about that they took it one step further. Everything with matter, had a soul.

Not a soul as in the sense the church teachers, a part of you that goes to God at death, but the part of you that lives on and transfers bodies at the next life. Each life we live, whether as a plant or animal, collects power.

It was during the lesson of learning how souls grow in power, that the topic of the ocean came up. Laken was told by his father, Rick that everything started as a sea urchin. A single cell organism that began to grow. It was from those initial growth moments at sea that caused the ocean to still be the most powerful driver of spells.

That's the reason why so many humans can 'find' water pipes when dowsing for them. It isn't because their bodies are made up of seventy-five percent water. It's because we are called to the water.

Everyone knows what balances the water out, the Earth's gravitational pull, that's affected by the sun and moon.

Seven days ago the solar eclipse happened. This was the catalyst, the point it all began. His coven, led by himself, had danced around the fire chanting spells of purification. Thanks to the wonderful networking abilities of the internet, covens across the globe had joined them in hopes of the first steps to rid the world of death and destruction. They all knew that if the world was allowed to continue on this path then it would certainly be destroyed. That's why it was up to Laken and his son Collins, to lead the way of the new order.

The Earth slowly had been trying to defend herself against humans. Fires, hurricanes, tidal waves, all sorts of natural disasters continued to pound on the humans but they had stood, resilient to the attempts. It was up to the covens to save her, to maintain the source of their power and free it of the souls who continued to consume her nutrients but never refilled her supply.

Their plan had taken a year for them to put together and coordinate across the globe. Collins had first made the comment as a joke to his father, that all the humans needed to be destroyed. But Laken wasn't joking, he was as evil as they got, and he was determined to make them pay for their misuse of the world.

One thing that all of the world knew, America was good for was meddling in affairs that weren't their own. In the nineteen nineties the United States of America's president at that time was William Jefferson Clinton. President Clinton had taken it upon himself to start studies on more vaccines to save the world population. Once again trying to thwart Mother Nature's attempt at saving herself. America had been up in arms over the human immunodeficiency virus, also referred to as HIV, outbreaks in Africa and that had been his legacy. Vaccinations across the globe. His administration had found a vaccine that would keep HIV away. In his final act as president he signed into law, a law that was also picked up by the World Health Organization and almost all of the civilized societies around the world. The new vaccine was now a requirement at the eighteen month checkup. No baby could opt out of it, even for religious reasons. That's how bad the crisis had become.

Even America had started taking away rights from infants.

Now every child who was born after January nineteenth two thousand and one had this vaccine immunity to the virus known as HIV.

Once Laken realized there was this similarity across the world his idea formed. This factoid made the curse easy to perform.

Taking a vile of blood from his son, a person who has both things required in his blood, the vaccine antibodies and the DNA for witches, Laken created a spell so powerful it would change the course of human history. He used the blood mixed with water and minerals his coven collected and used in spells during the solar eclipse. With the magical stirrings Mother Nature created during oceanic stores, mixing them all together during the hurricane was the perfect catalyst. With the powers of Mother Nature combined with the powerful blood from Collins veins, Laken was able to cast the death eater spell.

Within twenty-four hours of the spell being cast all of the humans who were over eighteen were dead, unless their blood contained the special genetic markers as Collins. All witches stemmed from the same blood line, they were all related in one way or another.

There were over two million people who contained the DNA markers for witch craft but only maybe half of them knew they were witches. It was truly a sad thing. They lived their lives in fear of being discovered. And Laken was tired of it. He had taken it upon himself to free the world of the judgement and oppression and the only way to achieve that was starting over.

Now was his time to shine, now it was his time for Collins to rise up. The father and son duo would lead the new world with their vision at the helm.

"Collins, prepare the coven." Laken said to his son.

"Yes father," Collins reached out and placed a simultaneous text notification that would trigger every member of the coven's cell phones he placed them on alert.

"Can you feel it son?" Laken had his arms raised and his eyes closed, face tilted towards the sun, soaking in her rays.

"What father?"

"The death. Everywhere. The souls are screaming out because they can't be reborn again. They are trapped. We've won."

Laken let the power around him fill his mind, he could see the humans he had taken in one quick spell. Their ghosts haunting the streets forever. "Better they haunt the streets as ghosts than take up the spots as humans." He told his son.

"How many are there?"

"Right now, in our presence, seventy. Across the world, billions."

"Collins you will see, come join hands, let me share the power with you."

While the two held hands and soaked in the power wafting in around them the rest of the world cried. Cried for the loss of the ones they loved. For the ones who they cherished, for the ones they admired.

Very few would make it out alive from this curse, and that was just what Laken wanted.

"My wife is waiting for me father."

"How can you tell that son?"

"Because I had a premonition. Sunny is out there, waiting for me to find her. But I will have to wait some time, for she is just a child now."

Present Day

"Father," Collins said, and he rushed into Laken's sitting room. Laken hated to be interrupted when he was thinking, and everyone knew that. Which told him Collins was willing to face potential death to deliver this message. "I have bad news Father."

Laken let his fingers tap along the table as he perused the plans of the attack scheduled for next week. They had taken out three compounds so far this year and were quickly depleting their supplies. Their coven had grown to four hundred members since August of last year and it was still growing.

"Spill it, what is your bad news Collins?"

"Sunny, she knows our names."

"How could she know that, she hasn't come into her powers completely yet." Laken's voice was loud and full of anger. He had warned Collins not to get attached to a child that they hadn't even met yet. His son's whole planned rested on the idea that this child would grow up to be his bride and they would take over.

"Father, now isn't the time to debate this."

"You're a fool!" Laken had stood from his chair and was now storming towards his son. "I told you to find a partner equal to you!"

Collins straightened up more, "She is equal and when she comes of age together we will be unstoppable."

"Men, I hate to interrupt," Laken looked over his shoulder to see his wife, Romania, walking towards them. "Need I remind you, Laken, that you're a good decade older than I am and look how we worked out."

"Romania, stay out of this. Your son made a decision and now he must live with that choice."

"I don't have to stay here and take this father I will go to her myself. I will explain to her what she would be, by my side."

"You will do nothing of the sort. We have our plans, in three weeks we will march onto this little community and take what is ours and destroy the rest." Laken began pacing his room, his attention now focused on the map of Florida they have posted on the wall.

"Laken, have you thought about my suggestion?" Romania had moved across the room and now was next to her husband. "If we go down there and simply talk to them, maybe this child will want to join on her own. We don't know, and war isn't always the solution. I keep telling you that the humans, even though they aren't magical, they are resources. We can still use them."

"Father, she's right."

"Silence!" Laken's voice bellowed throughout the room. He turned towards his son and stared him down as if his life depended on it. "Collins, you will go prepare the men and women. We are taking fifteen total that should be enough to bombard this colony of survivors. We leave for Saint Pete in two weeks. We will travel by foot. That should give us plenty of time. We don't want to exhaust our magical powers before we battle. Now go son, make me proud."

Collins bowed his head and left the room in silence. Laken knew his son, knew he was plotting his own mischievous feats. But that would have to wait for another day.

"Romania?"

"Yes Laken?" She walked to him and wrapped her arms around him.

"Let's retire for the night, I suddenly feel my energy shield weakening."

Collins was tired of his father's orders. He knew a thing or two about the world just like he did. His father constantly held it over his head that he was only seventeen and because of that he couldn't have any say in what went on. It had been his idea after all, the plans all started from his dream. It wasn't right or fair to be treated like a child.

He made his way through the hotel that he and his families' coven had taken up inside of. The main suites were reserved for Collins and his parents. The rest of their coven were scattered throughout the building and down into the streets. It was reassuring to know that there were hundreds of people willing to go to battle for you but that didn't give Collins comfort. He had hoped that his father would listen more. His own premonitions had been getting more powerful and he was certain now he could mentally connect with Sunny.

He had discovered two weeks ago in a dream finally that she was now aware of him. He had been dreaming of her for years now, he had seen her grow up in his mind's eye. It was creepy and weird, but he had come to accept it. Being a witch meant not having full control of your destiny. He hadn't discovered yet what made this little girl special, but he just knew something made it so.

"Sir, can we see you right away?" One of the other leaders of the coven had stopped him on his way to the hotel gym.

"Mr. Sean how can I help you today?"

"I was wondering if your father had finalized the invasion plans yet?"

Collins rubbed his face with his hand and sighed, "Yes he has, I don't agree with them still, but they are made."

"Good, the troops were getting anxious."

"That's actually where I was headed he wanted me to go work with the top fifteen, work on the strategy he has laid out."

"Good, I'll go with you then we can talk about what your father is planning."

Collins shook his head, "If it's all the same to you sir, I'd rather go alone."

He didn't wait for a response he just simply walked away. He was tired of everyone telling him what to do, he was going to start doing what he wanted. He was good enough to make the plan and good enough to come up with the idea then he was certainly good enough to work on his own.

Without taking any more time to mess around he stormed through the hotel and pushed open the gym doors.

"Our orders are here, we're invading the next community. Prepare for battle men, our future queen is about to be captured."

The End

Don't miss out!

Visit the website below and you can sign up to receive emails whenever Ashley Nemer publishes a new book. There's no charge and no obligation.

https://books2read.com/r/B-A-NDUF-SEBU

BOOKS 2 READ

Connecting independent readers to independent writers.

Did you love *The Ones Who Lived*? Then you should read *Maverick Touch The Cat* by Ashley Nemer!

Reporter Nadia Maverick takes an adventure through the underbelly of her town where she discovers that even the criminal life she had been reporting on isn't quite like it seemed. Things turn bad for Nadia when in the middle of an investigation the tables are turned and she becomes the one under the watchful eye of Mr. A. Everyone becomes a suspect when Nadia turns up missing. Who will be there to set her free? Read and see.

Read more at https://www.ashleynemer.com.

Also by Ashley Nemer

Kemah Sunrise
HoneySuckle Love

Maverick Touch
Maverick Touch The Cat
Maverick Touch The Highway
Maverick Touch The Adventure
Maverick Touch Jail Break

Novella & Short Stories
Bud's Christmas Wish / Miracle
Under The Moonlight
Wolf Pack

The Blood Series
Blood Purple

Blood Yellow
Blood Green
Blood White

The Ones
The Ones Who Lived

Watch for more at https://www.ashleynemer.com.

About the Author

Ashley is married and lives in Houston with her husband and their two children. She and her husband have been together for over a decade and he brings her more joy than she could ever imagine as a child. Their two children have filled their lives with laughter and excitement on a daily basis. She loves to read and has been hooked on the romance genre ever since her life long best friend Laura gave her "Ashes to Ashes' by Tami Hoag to read when they were in high school.

Ashley finds her strength through her family, especially her parents. They always support her in life, they push her to strive for greatness. There once was a motto that Ashley heard in her youth through her Taekwondo life 'Reach for the Stars' and that is what Ashley has always done. It was through her upbringing that the values Ashley has and display's came from. With her Parents always cheering her on in life she was able to grow up having faith in herself and her ability to conquer the world.Author Linkshttp://www.ashleynemer.comhttp://www.facebook.com/ashleynemer-authorhttp://www.facebook.com/ashers83 (Add Friend)http://ashleynemer.blogspot.comhttps://twitter.com/ashleynemerhttps://www.goodreads.com/user/show/2897381-ashley-nemer

Read more at https://www.ashleynemer.com.

ART OF SAFKHET

About the Publisher

SAFKHET READERSSafkhet's Pride - Our Street Team (Open to twenty (20) members)Here, readers will interact with the authors and have behind the scene chats to get the word out there about our book releases. We will have contests and special swag that is offered ONLY to our Street Team.Requirements: At least once a month post about one of the books released from The Art of Safkhet.At least once a month share one status by an author.When a new release comes out, recommend it to at least five friends on Goodreads.What's in it for you:All new releases the month they come out will be sold at a discount price. E-books will be 50% off and print books will be 30% off.When SWAG arrives all members will get first grabs at the itemsSpecial contests for print books or gift cards held just for members of the Street Team.Safkhet's Elite - Our Beta Readers (Open to fifty (50) readers only)Here, readers will get advanced readers copy (in e-book format) Readers will tell us which genre's they want to read and we will email them their ARC.Genres are:ParanormalContemporary RomanceEroticaScience FictionMysteryMythologyPoetryRequirements:Upon receiving an advanced copy of our new release, you will need to post your honest review with in fifteen days of its release and place a link to that review on the appropriate authors Facebook page.If you cannot read the ARC in a timely fashion please email Grace (info@artofsafkhet.com) so she can make note. Missing more than two e-book distributions in a row without reason will have you removed from Safkhet's Elite. Your review must be honest. We are not looking for all 5-Star reviews but honest opinions and thoughts about our work. By joining this program you agree to not share, distribute or sell the Advanced Readers Copy of our work. Some of you will want to be both, a Pride member and an Elite member. At this time we are asking that you pick one or the other. This may change in the future but for right now we ask that you just pick one. If you are interested in either of these please let us know. You can join Safkhet's Pride by going to this link https://www.facebook.com/groups/222253454608269/. This will take you to our Facebook group where we will post the different information. You can apply for Safkhet's Elite by commenting on this post with your name, email address and genre's you want to read and stating which of Ashley, Stacy, Anabella, or Niki books you liked most or by sending Grace an email at info@artofsafkhet.com with all of the information. Thank you for taking the time out to inquire about our new Readers Groups and we hope to see 70 new people in the near future!